BEAUTIFUL AND DARK

BY ROSA MONTERO

TRANSLATED FROM THE SPANISH BY ADRIENNE MITCHELL

D1057103

aunt lute books

san francisco

Aunt Lute Books
P.O. Box 410687
San Francisco, CA 94141
www.auntlute.com

Cover design: Amy Woloszyn, amymade.com
Text design: Amy Woloszyn, amymade.com

Senior Editor: Joan Pinkvoss
Managing Editor: Shay Brawn
Production: Noelle de la Paz, Soma Baral, Kara-Ann Young Ha Owens

Funding for the production of *Beautiful and Dark* was provided in part by a grant from the National Endowment for the Arts.

Library of Congress Cataloging-in-Publication Data

Montero, Rosa.
[Bella y oscura. English]
Beautiful and dark / by Rosa Montero ; translated from the Spanish by Adrienne Mitchell. -- 1st ed.
   p. cm.
ISBN 978-1-879960-82-4 (alk. paper)
I. Mitchell, Adrienne, 1975- II. Title.
PQ6663.O554B4513 2010
863'.64--dc22

                                   2010005820

Printed in the U.S.A. on acid-free paper

10 9 8 7 6 5 4 3 2 1

CHAPTER ONE

I was a witness to what I'm going to tell: the dwarf woman's betrayal, Segundo's murder, Star's arrival. It all took place in a distant era of my childhood that I am no longer sure if I remember or invent: because then, the sky and earth had not been severed yet, and everything seemed possible to me. The universe had just been created, as Grandmother Barbara had made a point of telling me. "When I was born," she said, "the world began." Since I was young and she was already very old, that seemed like a very, very long time ago.

To start my story somewhere, I'll say that my life began on a train trip, my life as I remember and recognize it, and prior to which I keep only a handful of disconnected, cloudy images, as if they were blurred by the dust of the tracks, or perhaps darkened by the last tunnel the locomotive went through before it came to the final stop. So, as I recall, I was born out of that tunnel's blackness, daughter of the clamor and clatter of the tracks, birthed from the entrails of the earth on a cold April afternoon at an enormous and desolate station.

We made our way into that station, blowing and screeching, while the dead tracks multiplied on both sides of the car and writhed and jumped, and neared the windows, and moved away again with a sudden start, like the taught elastic rope of that girls' game that I had probably played at some time or other in the ancient time that I no longer remember, nor want to remember.

All the travelers got off the train before me, driven by their routine anxiety, so that they seemed to be fleeing instead of walking. I watched their backs disappear on the platform ahead, those backs with their overcoats and raincoats, the women and men who had been so interested in me during the journey, who had asked me questions, and offered me chocolate and candies, and caressed my cheeks amicably. And now their backs were further and further away, industriously dragging suitcases. They left me alone, the train already dead and quiet behind me, a dome of dark iron and dirty windows above me, and a gray sidewalk that gave off an unpleasant frozen breath below me. My legs were naked between my white socks and the spread of my skirt, and they shivered from the cold.

Then a blue shadow stooped over my head and enveloped me in a sweet and sticky perfume.

"Hi ... It's you, right?"

I didn't know how to answer. She smelled like violets.

"Well of course it's you, what a stupid question ..." continued the woman hastily, "I'm Amanda. Do you remember me? No, of course not, how are you going to remember if you were so small when they took you ... I'm your Aunt Amanda, your uncle's wife... Before, years ago, we lived together. Before they took you to the orphanage. Your mother and I were good friends. Do you remember your mother? Oh, I probably shouldn't talk to you

I didn't know who they were, but I didn't dare ask either. Girls don't ask questions, especially if they come from where I did. So we began to walk, Amanda at a good clip with me dangling from one of her hands and my suitcase from her other. It was the first time I saw a city so busy, bewildering, and brilliant. It didn't seem real: it was an open-air fair, intoxicatingly golden. The sidewalks were adorned with stone baskets full of natural flowers, and the store windows followed one after the other, replete with indescribable treasures, and bursting with lights. Then there were the people, all those men and women who came and went with rustling packages in their hands, rustling smiles, rustling suits, all of them rustling from the crowns of their heads to the tips of their fine shoes, as if they were new, people making a debut, not a thing about them worn out. All of them, everybody, even though there were many of them, lived in that marvelous city, and undoubtedly had shiny new houses and were happy. And then I began to think that perhaps we had a pretty house to go to, and that surely we were about to arrive, because the blue sky was fading, night was falling, and I knew that girls couldn't be out at night. So at every corner we turned, I said to myself, "this will be it." But it never was and we kept on walking.

We walked so much that the shop windows became scarce, and there were no more stone baskets with flowers. Already there weren't as many lights as before, and the air was bluish like my pleated skirt. 'Baba,' I said to myself, 'Baba, I hope we arrive soon.' I began to feel tired. The houses were all the same and pretty, with white moldings that looked like meringue. And there were lots of trees, and at every tree a sniffing dog, and next to each one a man or a woman, a boy or a girl. The city around here wasn't an outdoor fair anymore, but instead a clean and still place, with

about that either ... What a fool I am, you see, I'm a little ner
OK, well here we are..."

She had spoken all at once, without taking a breath. S
a frightened expression on her face. She lifted her hand up
mouth and left it there for a few moments, limp and dangli
she were about to bite her fingernails and had changed her
the last second. She was young, with very round eyes and fle
cheeks. She was wearing a long light-blue coat and a little
that looked homemade. She looked at me, smiled, shuffle
around on the ground, and cleared her throat: she was the
indecision. Finally she stooped down and lifted my sma
effortlessly.

"Good, it doesn't weigh much ... I'm glad because w
walk a while. Well, we better go, don't you think?"

She grabbed me by the hand the same way that she ha
the suitcase, squeezing tightly, as if I were going to slip
fingers. We crossed the platform, passed through son
doors, and plunged into the central vestibule and its
uproar of loudspeakers and shouts. Amanda adva
the crowds of people, ducking and squeezing my ha
Another pair of automatic doors opened before us, and
burst we found ourselves on the street. The city exten
as blinding as a fire. Crystal towers, luminous, and
windows, hypnotizing colored ads. Above, I saw a lit
sky and the sparkling of windows set on fire by the a

"So many lights..." I exclaimed, admiringly.

"It's pretty, isn't it?" answered Amanda with
area, the city is very pretty. Of course, I don't re
well anyway. I got here the day before yesterday a
tomorrow. But let's go before it gets dark."

6

exquisite streets on which it seemed easy to be happy. Everybody was preparing to eat dinner. The entire city was unfolding their napkins noisily, and darkness was approaching definitively, the secret night: adult and uninhabitable. Amanda picked up the pace, and I followed her. The dogs, the trees, the windows with creamy lace curtains and warm light were being left behind.

We skirted around ultra-black parks that had already been devoured by shadows; we crossed streets that seemed like highways; we left the streetcar lines behind. When had the people disappeared? I looked back and ahead, and I couldn't see anyone. There wasn't a single shop around, and all the doors were closed off. I tripped; the ground wasn't level anymore, and there were potholes, crumbling stones, cracks. On the opposite sidewalk an illuminated but empty gas station appeared, its sheet metal ad for oil creaking in the wind. I glanced at Amanda; under the cold neon light she looked pale and strange, with her mouth clamped shut and her stare fixed. We left the station behind and with every step the shadows got thicker. Now it was really nighttime, and there were no more cars driving by in the street.

The houses we were passing now were abandoned and ruined. There were boarded-up windows with cracked panes. Doors blocked off with cardboard. Peeling walls. Black warehouses with broken roofs. The air smelled like urine and tasted like iron on your lips. Someone appeared on a corner. A gray shadow leaning against the wall. Amanda's hand squeezed mine, and we walked a little faster. The shadow smiled at us as we passed by; Amanda didn't look, but I did. It was a big woman that looked like a man. Or maybe it was a man that looked like a woman. Pants, raincoat and shoulders as wide as a boxer. With gaudy, blond hair, full of curls, a lot of make-up, and thin lips, the color of blood. I looked back. There in the background, faraway, the gas station seemed to float, like a phantom, in the neon's greenish glow.

We crossed the sidewalk and turned at the next corner: the echo of our footsteps was deafening in the silence. It started to drizzle. The street was a dark tunnel; the shadows swayed next to the scarce, weak streetlights. The night extended over the world like a huge spider web: in some corner the spider would lie in wait, with hairy legs, hungry and ready for us. We were walking more and more quickly. Amanda went on with her head down, as if ready to charge. I was running a little and panting, and my chest was weighing down on me. The damp, cold air entered my lungs painfully, as if a long nail were driving into my side. The streetlights made the wet ground shine once in awhile: it was a somber reflection as if the thick, oily shadows were melting the asphalt.

Suddenly a man appeared before us, out of nowhere, from the darkness. He approached with his hands open and arms extended, like the monsters in bad dreams. I squeezed my eyelids closed and thought, 'Baba, I hope he goes away, I hope he disappears, Baba, Babita, I hope nothing happens to me' ... but I looked up, and he was still there. Dressed in rags, with a stubbly beard, and watery eyes as if he were crying. But he was smiling. Amanda jerked suddenly, changing direction; we dodged him as fish dodge each other at the last moment in their narrow fish tanks. And the man was left behind us muttering words that I couldn't understand, while we walked fast, very fast, without running, because running would have been succumbing to the danger. We just walked as fast as we could with our hearts between our teeth, pursued by the resounding beat of our own steps.

We turned down a new street, and there were lights. But they weren't like the ones before, like the sparkling of the beautiful city downtown; these were a few handfuls of naked light bulbs, grouped here and there over some doors. Close up they blinded and dazzled you, but as soon as you got four steps the shadows trapped you again. They seemed as if they were meant to stun, not to illuminate. We went up the street, and strange men were saying things to us. They stood below the lights and invited us in. Smoke and a reddish glow, the breath of hell, came out through the half-open doors. Amanda's heels rang out on the damp cobblestones; my heart beat quickly inside my chest. We went further and further up the street, looking ahead, as if the men didn't exist, and they yelled, murmured, laughed, and stretched out their devilish claws toward us. The street became more and more steep, and my legs were as heavy as rocks; it was vertigo of lights and shadows. And the heat of the lights dried my tears.

Suddenly, when I least expected it, we went through a door and up a narrow wooden staircase. On the second floor, there was a counter and an old woman with a lot of make-up.

"Number two," said Amanda with a hoarse voice, out of breath.

A few locks of hair had escaped from under her knit cap, and they were stuck to her flushed face; I don't know if it was because of the rain or the sweat. She didn't look good, but the old made-up woman looked at us without interest and handed her the key with a bored gesture. Amanda hurled herself down the hall ahead of me. She stopped at a door, dropped my suitcase on the floor, unlocked the door and opened it. We entered; she shut it, locked both bolts and leaned against the door with a deep sigh. She was trembling.

She let go of my hand, and I realized that it was wet and very warm. I dried it surreptitiously on my skirt while I contemplated the room. It was a small room with two big beds that left little space.

The walls were papered with a brown flowery design, and there was a very dirty orange-colored shag rug on the floor. Behind the door there was a small sink that seemed new. To the side a rickety dresser with some round holes where the handles should have been. Suddenly something roared and cracked in the air above our heads, and the windowpanes rattled.

"Don't worry, it's just an airplane. We're right next to the airport," explained the woman.

We were silent as we listened to the booming in the sky get further and further away.

"Now that I think of it, are you hungry? Over there is some cheese and a little bread, and, look what I've got for later! Chocolate!" said Amanda with a liveliness that sounded fake. She took a bar out of her pocket.

I took the chocolate, above all because she wanted me to take it. She smiled, pleased. She took off her knit cap and then her coat; she was wearing black pants and a blue jersey; she was very thin. Her round face and pudgy cheeks seemed to promise a fuller body, but she was very fragile, bony, straight, with narrow shoulders and slender wrists. She dried off her damp hair with the lining of her coat and then she let herself fall onto the bed with a gasp.

"I'm exhausted."

I would have liked to have asked her what we were doing there, who we were waiting for, what my life was going to be like, but instead of doing that, I went to the window and opened the curtains.

"I don't know, I thought it would take less time to get here. I got lost; I was frightened ... I don't know the city very well anyway..." she mumbled.

I didn't open my mouth. Amanda then sat up on the bed and stared directly at me.

"You know what?" she said slowly, "All trips end up, sooner or later, turning into a nightmare."

I looked out the window. The street was dark, the asphalt wet. And in the background, the lights, the men, the enormity of the world.

CHAPTER TWO

In a few days I learned the rules of the Neighborhood. During the daylight, there were children, elderly people dressed in black who walked dragging their feet, little grocery stores stocked with canned goods and jugs of detergent, corner bars with Formica tables and crippled cats in the Neighborhood. Planes were buzzing overhead like hornets in August; they were silvery, shiny, and potbellied, and they appeared and disappeared between the clouds thrusting their noses in the sky and letting themselves fall almost on top of us over the earth, so close that sometimes one could see the landing gear. They were a great booming shadow that ran above the streets.

But at nightfall, the light bulbs came on, and those mysterious doors that had been closed all day long opened—a vertiginous labyrinth of shadows and corners. At night, I was told, it wasn't good to go out alone, and especially near Casas Chicas, which was just at the edge of the Neighborhood where everything ended. There was also a street where I was forbidden to go; I called it Violet Street because at night a strange and dismal purple-red glow emerged from the windows. I glimpsed that radiance one afternoon from the corner; Amanda, who was walking behind me, grabbed me by the hand and told me, "Don't look." But from the corner there was nothing to see: just the sloping street and that sickly light.

There was an asphalt street that led to the high square in the neighborhood, which was a large open space with a few cafes around. Further the streets were simple lanes with small houses, grass and earth, like a country town. And even further, at the end were the dumps and Casas Chicas.

"I already found out about everything," Chico told me one day. Our area goes to the High Square. Going further than that becomes dangerous right away. In spite of being much younger than me—just a little boy Chico—had a very fitting understanding of the place's rules, yet he, too, was a new arrival to the city. But he came from another Neighborhood, and all neighborhoods, he told me, were the same.

We were seated on the curb, across from the apartment building, and he clutched his legs with his arms and supported his face on his pointy knees. Chico was Amanda's son, and he was just like her, but more: even more fragile, even more pale, the bulk of his face and his body even more disproportionate. All of his body was a yellowish color, including his hair: and only his large, floppy ears offered a delicate, revealing outline with a pinkish hue. Those ears were the only things that were truly alive on his face; they seemed like the quivering wings of a butterfly about to flutter.

"And two very important things: one, never tell strangers anything, and the other, if you hear noises at night, don't get out of bed..." Chico continued explaining, cradling his legs on the curb.

He looked happy because he knew more than I did. He came with *them* a day after us, just as Amanda had announced. And there were two of: Grandmother Barbara and Segundo. Amanda was trembling when they arrived, so I learned to fear them before meeting them.

It happened like this: Amanda and I were still sleeping when someone pounded on the door of the room. Amanda stood up in one single leap and flung her blue coat on, flustered. Her hands trembled, and the coat slipped off her shoulders twice before she managed to fasten the top button. She unlocked the bolts awkwardly, taking much longer than necessary, as the blows on the wood intensified. I, still half-asleep, thought—I don't know why—that there was a large, wild animal on the other side of the door; and if it managed to get in the room, it would crush us. But Amanda had finished with the latches; now she opened the door and stood aside. Leaving me alone and naked in that immense bed.

She entered the room like a cold wind. The surrounding air crackled - I don't know if it was an airplane or her very presence. The room was still in shadows; the hallway intensely lit. At first the only thing I saw was her formidable and dark silhouette outlined against a background of fire; and a hand that clenched a shaft and the thunder high above. I covered my face with the sheet; I think I shrieked. I felt, in a an instant of terror, someone was grabbing me by the shoulder and dragging me out from under my mask. Against the light I saw before me: a hooked nose, some shiny eyes, a necklace of cold pearls hissing between lace.

"Enough nonsense," said a hard mouth that seemed made to give orders. "Those tricks are not going to work here."

Nevertheless there was something in her tone that calmed me a little: a power so absolute that she had no need to hurt me. The woman scrutinized me in silence for a few moments and what she saw seemed to please her. She peacefully closed her eyes halfway, her gaze buried in a well of wrinkles. She caressed the pearls; they sounded like the sea, like water through pebbles.

"I am your Grandmother, Grandmother Barbara. You wouldn't remember me. From now on, I'm in charge of you, and you have to do everything I say. Do you understand me? I'm the one who gives orders here."

She seemed to wait for something, so I nodded my head hurriedly. She looked at me attentively again, and something about me pleased her again. That was a comfort. She lifted my chin, clicked her tongue.

"You look more and more like your father," she said.

And she turned around and left the room.

On that occasion, the first meeting, I didn't even notice Segundo's presence. Because back then, before he had the scar, Segundo was barely visible when he was next to Grandmother Barbara. But yes I did see Chico, who slipped into the room after the old woman left and hugged his mother laughing and chattering happily. It seemed strange to me that Amanda had a child, because she hadn't told me, and I think it also seemed strange that she had been separated from him, that she hadn't had him with her the night before. But I didn't find out the reason for that separation until much later. It was one of the many things that Chico didn't know how to explain to me that morning when we were seated on the curb, him embracing his skinny legs while he taught me about the rules of the Neighborhood. As for the rest, they were simple; most of all they depended on knowing one's own place and acting accordingly.

CHAPTER THREE

Amanda informed me right away, as soon as Segundo and Grandmother Barbara arrived, that the dwarf woman had yet to arrive, so my Grandmother appeared somewhat anxious. Grandmother had a great big calendar on the wall with a neat, pretty drawing of a dark blue sea with a ray of sun painted over the water, and every morning she crossed off the date with an impatient stroke of her thick red pencil.

I asked Amanda who the dwarf woman was, and she didn't know, or perhaps she didn't want to answer me.

She limited her words to, "She is a very odd, very intelligent person."

And when I would insist, she repeated the same thing, "You'll see soon. You'll meet her. An extremely odd woman."

One of those first nights, when we were already staying alone in our own room (Chico and I slept together in a room with two beds), he came over to me on his tip toes, and proposed a deal.

"You make my bed for one month, and I will show you something that belongs to the dwarf woman."

"What is it?"

"Some written papers. Something very good. It's a bargain."

"OK."

Chico took out some papers from under his mattress. Later, when I was making his bed all those weeks, I found that he kept a heap of different objects under the mattress: tiny, prized matchbox cars, a little blue plastic binder full of papers, two or three belt buckles, a broken brooch, and a handful of shiny buttons. But that night he only took out a few yellowing pages from the binder, and he held them out for me with a grand gesture. It seemed to be a letter, an old letter written by the dwarf woman to an unknown recipient.

"Read it out loud," said Chico because he didn't know how to read yet, and he wanted to find out what it said. So we sat on the floor, and we put the lamp on the rug between us so that its glow could not be seen from the hall. And, in whispers, I read the letter that was, in fact, the first tale I heard about Airela., It read like this:

My dear,

I miss you so much that I'm living with half an imagination, half a heart, half of my ideas and feelings, like a drunk who is at the point of losing consciousness halfway between wakefulness and passing out, or like a dying person with one foot in this world and the other foot already placed in the black nothingness. I'm trying to say that I'm half a person without you, just a speck, a scrap of flesh and nerves standing on end yearning for the being that completes me. That's why I'm writing you, even knowing that you will never even be able to read these lines; words create worlds, and now they are capable of creating, as I'm writing to you, the consoling illusion of your presence for me.

Once I met a man - I don't know if you know about it – who was my mentor in the art of speaking. This happened a long time ago, when I was very young, and in a remote corner of the Adriatic, on the border of what is Albania today. A time and a place very favorable for mystery, for credulity and for magic, and not like here now. My mentor was what today would be called a carnival charlatan, but then he entertained and taught people, and people trusted him. I worked to lure people for him; we would arrive at the market squares and I would do some cartwheels and two or three flips because I was a good acrobat in my youth. The show attracted onlookers, and once a big circle of spectators had gathered, my mentor began with his art. He was a very good narrator: as soon as he opened his mouth the whole world became captivated by his words. He told sweet stories of young lovers and cruel stories of ambitious knights; very ancient stories that men and women like him had repeated century after century; or stories he invented as he went along. At the end, after the stories, he sold something. Chalk scrapings mixed with sand, which he said was moon dust and that scattered on the threshold of the house, worked to keep misfortune from entering; or some pretty colored feathers that belonged to a phoenix bird that one had to put under the pillow at night to avoid bad dreams. When what I'm going to tell you now happened, he was selling some rings. We had a lot; an old artisan had made them very cheaply in a distant city. They were some bronze rings set with a black, unpolished stone. They weren't pretty or good, but the people paid for them as if they were because they believed they were dealing with a magic stone.

Do you know the old legend of Charlemagne and the enchanted ring? That was the story my mentor told them before selling them the rings. Charlemagne, being already very old, fell hopelessly in love with a peasant girl whom he married and made his queen. He loved her so much, and the old emperor was so dazzled by his love, that he began to neglect his official responsibilities, thus tarnishing his dignified and respected life. Then the girl died suddenly; Charlemagne ordered that they put her in a decorated room, and he closed himself in with the body day and night. The kingdom was abandoned; the subjects astonished. Alarmed by the excess and suspecting a spell, the archbishop Turpin entered the mourning room and searched the body furtively, and in fact, he found a magic ring under the girl's tongue and took it out. Charlemagne lost all interest in the deceased girl at once, but he fell entrancingly in love with the archbishop. Upset and scandalized by the emperor's passion, the archbishop cast the ring into the bottom of Lake Constance. And the old emperor spent the rest of his days sitting on the damp hillsides contemplating the lake. It's a sad story as you can see. In that lake alight with the dim, fading rays of the setting sun is the portrait of desires that are never attained. My mentor told the legend very well. Some afternoons as he told his story, I cried. And that was before I had even met you, you who are my lake.

After talking of Charlemagne my mentor took out his rings. He was a very bright man, and he knew that a ring that was too powerful would be terrifying. He didn't say, consequently, that the rings were like that of the poor emperor, a magnet for hearts and hopes. He explained that Charlemagne's ring and the ones he was selling had the same stone, which was a rock split by lightening one moonless night; and the material radiated the power and energy of that shaft. Sorcerers used those lively stones to make magic rings that worked for one marvel or another, depending on the incantation that had been consecrated. My mentor's rings possessed an honest quality, and when they felt near an evil person, with blood on their hands, the ring's black stone began to sweat. He sold a lot of pieces. Everyone wanted to know who they were dealing with.

One night, in a small provincial city, the police came to where we were sleeping. They were very brusque. We found out, once we were at the police station, that an old woman's throat had been slit, and a good malachite and gold necklace had been stolen from her. The deceased's neighbor saw the thief leave and was sure that it was my mentor who he had seen a couple of days earlier at the market. There was no more proof than that testimony; the necklace never appeared, nor the knife from the crime, nor a drop of blood on the accused's clothing. But the neighbor had bought one of the rings, and when he went to the police station to make the identification and my mentor drew near, the ring's stone began to sweat and it pearled into a transparent water. The judge didn't formally admit the sign as evidence, but everyone was convinced that the ring had signaled the murderer. That surely influenced his condemnation to death, such that one could say my mentor lost his life to his own eloquence. I went to visit him the last night, and then they gave me his belongings because he didn't have friends or relatives. They told me that he had spent the last hours calmly reading a book and that when they came to get him to go up to the gallows, he made a sign between the pages to mark the place where he was reading. I later received the book: it was a French edition of *One Thousand and One Nights* and it had, in fact, a corner folded between two stories. I still keep the volume and the mark. For a narrator like him, folding that page with so much integrity faced with nothing ahead of him, was a dignified way to die and a very elegant gesture. That's what I would like: to die my own death, to know how to end it with a certain grandeur. Since we came to the world as animals – bloody and blind, useless and irrational – we'll leave this life as humans with notable and symbolic deaths. We are the heroes of the narration of our lives because what differentiates us from inferior creatures is that we are capable of telling our stories and even inventing our own existence for ourselves. From this side of the words, at last, without a ring, without a lake, and without patience, desperate from your absence, writing you to remember you, your

Airelai.

CHAPTER FOUR

One day Segundo went to talk to the woman at the counter, the one who gave out the keys; I saw him lean on the wood with its peeling paint while she looked at him with a suspicious and surly expression. Segundo said something; I didn't hear him, and the old lady shook her head. Then he placed a wad of bills on the table, and then another. The woman hurried to grab them; she ran her fingers through her yellowing, dried out curls; came out of her hole, smiled, and she left. That's how we ended up with the whole boarding house. We must have been rich.

Grandmother Barbara lived in two big rooms that were connected by an archway; they had once been a dance school and still had a wooden bar and a cracked mirror on one of the walls. Next there was the room full of cats; the one with the couch that Segundo used as a living room, and two more that were kept under lock and key. Chico and I stayed in the same bedroom where I spent the first night, the one with the filthy orange carpet; Segundo and Amanda, Chico's parents, slept across the hall right next to the room with the couch, in a big, decrepit room. Sometimes one could hear them shouting, followed by choked up cries. At those times, Chico got in bed, clenched his fists and shut his eyes tight. And he would say, "I'm sleeping. I am completely asleep." Even if that happened in the middle of the day with the sun flooding in through the window with its breath of glowing dust.

But Chico wasn't the only one to get into bed. Grandmother Barbara also spent most of her time sprawled out on her enormous black wooden bed that she had had set up in her rooms. She said that this way, she wouldn't get worn out and, therefore, she would live forever. One day I asked her how old she was, and she told me she was as old as eternity. "When I was born, the world began."

From that I deduced that she had experienced the great flood, Noah's Ark, and the three Wise Men. That news amazed me, but to tell the truth, it didn't surprise me. Grandmother Barbara was so wise, so strong, so grand; it didn't seem extraordinary that she had seen everything. She was a very tall, robust woman; the bones of her face were strong and prominent and seemed poorly connected from one to the next, such that the right side of her face was very different from the left, even though both proved to be equally fierce. Her nose was long and hooked, her eyes small, golden, and very intense. She would have had the face of a raptor if it were not for her great asymmetrical jaw.

She always dressed in an imposing manner even when she was lying down, and she sat on her bed like a queen on her cushioned throne; she wasn't resting, but rather on display. Her dresses crunched with the slightest movement; they were heavy clothes made of taffeta and silk, velvet and brocade, in dark green, deep ocean blue, or the color of dried blood red; she wore her stark white hair pulled back tightly in a perfect bun. Around her bed, over the nightstands, the flames from her oil lamps bounced, and the smoke from her incense sticks swirled around. She looked like a goddess in her chapel, and that is why the only time that I went into the old church in the neighborhood, I thought that the old gold reredos, shining in the shadows behind the main altar with its perfumed and dripping candles, its carnations, and Virgin in the middle, was nothing other than a shrine to Grandmother Barbara, a remembrance of her power and glory.

That immense woman would send for me once in awhile. She made me come into her room, and I went to her with my teeth chattering. Then she would order me to sit at the foot of her bed, and she would offer me exquisite pine nut pastries. We would talk a little, or, to be precise, she would talk. Sometimes she told me things that I didn't understand, and sometimes she would ask ridiculous questions: "Are you OK?" "Yes, Grandmother." "Do you need something?" "No, Grandmother." But at other times, she would remain so still and quiet that she seemed to be sleeping, and I wouldn't even dare to nibble the cookies to keep from making noise.

Then, at night, Chico would ask me to tell him what Grandmother had said. Because Grandmother Barbara never sent for him; she seemed to ignore him completely. This seemed normal to Chico because no one paid much attention to him, but some time later, the dwarf woman would tell us that it was not Chico's fault but rather his father's. It was his father, Segundo, who Grandmother Barbara was trying to torment by not welcoming his son. Chico liked that explanation so much, and he would often ask, with an innocent expression, why Grandmother didn't ask to see him.

"Because Grandmother Barbara cannot stand her son, that is, this son, and she could never stand him. That's a matter of fact. And you have the bad luck of having Segundo as a father," the dwarf woman repeated patiently for the thousandth time.

"Ah..." Chico would always say, captivated.

When they arrived, Amanda told me that Segundo was a magician. And that he made objects appear and disappear, and he would cut a person into seven pieces. I never saw him work, nor did I see his magical powers, nor did he have colored chests or the pretty clothes I had seen on magicians on TV. And about cutting someone into seven pieces; yes, I did believe he was capable of that, but I highly doubted that he could then repair the damage. The only thing Segundo seemed to do was spend half his time in the neighborhood bars and the other half snoozing in his bedroom. He would sleep during the day, and in the evening, he would go into the bathroom and take a long time; at last he would come out, freshly shaved, with his perfect jacket and a very clean shirt, throwing punches and glancing sideways at himself in the mirror behind the sink while he went through the door.

Sometimes strange people came to visit. In the afternoons and even at night, Chico and I were woken more than once by the racket of voices and steps. At those times, Chico would always tell me, "Don't get up." And he would cover his big ears with the pillow. But one dawn when they were laughing a lot, I got out of bed on my tip toes and edged open the door. I saw them conversing in the back, standing at the end of the hallway: they were either coming or going. Two men in jackets, two shrill girls, and Segundo. I was gazing at them for quite some time; they seemed to be talking to each other about very funny things. Suddenly one of the guys turned and looked toward me; he was short, dark, dressed in black, with a lip curled up by a scar and eyebrows that were very close together. I shuddered. The hallway was lit, but my room was dark, and I had only cracked the door; he couldn't see me. Or perhaps he could? I didn't dare move so that I wouldn't give myself away, and I stayed like that, still as stone, for a very long time. The group was talking and laughing, and the man was looking at me; and through the small triangle that the scar opened in his mouth, I could see a shining gold tooth.

Finally they left, and the slice of light that slipped past the edge of the door went out. I went back to bed and dreamt that the man with cut lips was chasing me, and then about the large, cold, dismal house where they locked us up -- children who didn't have parents. I woke up crying, like many other early mornings; and that time, too, like the other times, I could only find consolation repeating, "Baba," my secret word, which came from the depths of my infancy, and whose meaning, if it had one, I no longer remembered. And so, I clenched my fists and closed my eyes tight, and I muttered franticly, "Baba, Baba." Like a litany against darkness' misery, "Baba, little Baba, Baba." And that meaningless word relieved my sadness and left a sweet taste in my mouth.

In Grandmother Barbara's room, on the little table on the right side, there were two big, framed photos. Two photos of men. One was older, with big, wide blue eyes; he didn't have an unpleasant face, but there was something frightening about his expression. And the other one was young, dark, with light eyes as well, and pronounced cheekbones and thick lips. One day, Grandmother Barbara grabbed that portrait, showed it to me, and said, "This is Maximo, your father." "Where is he?" I dared to ask. And she only answered, "He will return. I know he will return."

And since that time I had the absolute certainty that my father would, sooner or later, come for me.

CHAPTER FIVE

In most instances Chico was invisible. That is, even if he were in front of you, you wouldn't see him. He possessed a unique ability to remain still and quiet, as if hidden or evaporating into thin air. He cowered and shrunk; and he spent hours that way, curled up in a ball, sitting on the stoop by the doorway. He didn't have friends and almost never played. He would just sit on his stair waiting for someone to arrive to ask him to do something. Because Chico ran errands. He hunted flies for Mariano, the bartender's, turtle. At breakfast time and mid afternoon, he brought coffees up for the women who worked at night. He was a messenger and delivered packages. He spent his days coming and going. Neither of us went to school.

With his little jobs, Chico earned a few coins, and when he gathered a handful, he would spend them on matchbox cars and candies. He usually would buy them at Rita's store, which had a neon light on the wall behind the counter so that Rita was always backlit against the light. Still she could be seen clearly. She was a large, middle-aged woman with a big bust and enormous arms that came out from either side of her thorax and stuck out like crab's claws. They used to say in the neighborhood that one winter day Rita had killed a man who had tried to assault her. The guy put the point of a knife between her breasts, and then she grabbed a hammer and smashed his head with one blow, like someone cracking open a ripe watermelon. Even though some maintained that the deceased was not a thief, but rather an old friend, and that he wasn't going to rob her, but rather, long ago, he had already taken something from her – something that was valuable but not tangible. But they said all this in whispers with great care because Rita was married to Juan the Pighead, who was a brute. And, for talking too much, more than one person had been found dead with his mouth sewn shut with a wire amidst the hovel of the Casas Chicas shantytown.

I saw Chico coming from Rita's store one afternoon, loaded with paper bags. He was a boy who knew how to be generous when he had plenty, and right away he handed me a packet of mints magnanimously. The two of us sat down on the stoop chewing our sweets.

"Rita says there is a guy in the neighborhood who is asking for us."

"For us? For you and me? Someone from the neighborhood?" I was frightened.

"For all of us. Some outsider. Rita doesn't know him."

And I suddenly thought: it could be my father. "But he asked for me? For me specifically?"

"Well, yes." Chico was surprised. "Odd, right? He asked for Grandmother Barbara. And for Segundo. And for you. Rita didn't like him."

It had to be him. Who else would be interested in me? It had to be him.

"And he was dark with light eyes and thick lips..." I ventured, eager.

"I don't know. Rita didn't like him. Rita told me, 'Chico, tell your family that they're out looking for you.' "

"Wait. Don't tell anyone yet. I'll inform Grandmother Barbara tomorrow." I said; I'm not sure why: perhaps because I had a premonition, without knowing it, about Segundo's relationship with my father.

"Okay," Chico agreed quickly.

I didn't think having to speak with Segundo was very appealing to him. He always referred to his father that way, with Segundo's name, or he would simply say "he." He would never say, "my father." The boy meticulously split a licorice twist and gave me half. We were chewing it for a long while in calm silence until, suddenly, I noticed that Chico was keeping still and was beginning to assume the color of the stoop.

"What's wrong?"

I turned, and I saw them come down the street toward us: three boys about fourteen or fifteen years old. Looking more closely, I saw that one was Buga. I stood up and pretended to be taking something out of the mangled, rusty mailbox. I had never had a clash with Buga, but everyone knew he was cocky.

"Hey, buddies, look who's here: the snotty big-ears," said Buga in high spirits.

And he approached Chico smiling. I had no doubt who they came looking for because the boy was already the same color as the wall, and he was perfectly invisible except that he really could be found.

"Let's see, you snotty, filthy, kid with big-ears: what do we have today?"

Chico, trembling, handed him the candies that were left. Buga inspected them opening the wrappers.

"And that's it? Well, hell...." He said in a lively manner, putting a handful of mints into his mouth, "today you've scoffed it all down, huh, little twerp..."

"No... I didn't buy much, no ... I didn't have money," stammered the boy.

"Oh, no?" Let's see," said Buga.

He grabbed Chico and in no time at all he had him upside down, hanging from his ankles; he shook him like that a few times, with the boy screaming and his two friends cracking up with laughter. I couldn't help it and took a step toward them.

"Leave him alone already," I said softly. And immediately I regretted having spoken.

But unfortunately for me, they had heard.

"What? What is that lice-ridden girl saying?" Buga asked one of his friends, as if he could not stoop to speak to me.

"To leave him alone already, she says" repeated the other.

Buga let go of Chico, who fell on his head on the ground. The blow resounded and must have hurt, but the boy remained still on the ground, just the way he fell, without crying or moving, trying to acquire the texture and coloration of the pavers.

"Well we left him alone. That's it. Left alone."

He came toward me, and I felt the pressure of the wall by the stoop at my back. Buga was short and strong with a husky face and thick slanted eyelids, almost without eyelashes. His breath smelled like mint, and his feet, which were crammed into some dirty gym shoes, smelled of sweat. He pinned me against the wall and began to mumble, irked.

"And, you, where did you come from? And who told you that you could talk, filthy slut, and why are you shouting?"

I wasn't shouting. To tell the truth I don't think that I was even breathing. Baba, I hope he doesn't hurt me.

"You'll see ..."

Then he lifted up my skirt and put his hand inside my panties. I felt his rough, warm fingers for a few moments searching down there. A pinch. I shrieked. Buga took his hand out.

"She's just a little brat. She doesn't even have hair," he said with a voice full of disdain, "Let's get away from here."

And they went away, but not without knocking Chico, who was still on the ground, with a sideways kick, a weak jab that was not vicious, a simple reminder of who they were. I went to Chico, and I helped him get up; his nose was bleeding, and he had a welt on his cheek. I stroked his head, satisfied for having intervened.

"Poor kid, I'm so sorry. Thank goodness I was here with you."

The boy looked at me, scowling and sullen while he stopped the bleeding with the edge of his sweater.

"Thank goodness? It was all your fault..." he grumbled.

"Oh yeah?" I was annoyed. "Well, don't worry, I will never ever help you again."

"You haven't helped me! I don't want you to help me! You don't know anything! You're a girl."

I was speechless.

"That's how things are. Don't you understand?" Chico went on. "They come, and they make fun of me a little, but I comply, and they don't hurt me."

"Oh, no? Look at your face."

"Because you screwed up; it's all your fault; you don't understand the neighborhood."

"But, then, what about you? You don't mind if they knock you upside down and insult you?"

Chico crossed his arms.

"When they come, I let them eat my candies and push me. These guys and other ones. The ones who are stronger. That's how things are. And it's fine, it doesn't matter to me. But I wouldn't want to be like them either. You see? They—the strong guys— have to be beating each other up all the time. Really getting into it, with knives and the like. But I just have to put up with a little shove. It's not bad. It's nothing to worry about."

He took his sweater away from his nose; it wasn't bleeding anymore.

"The insults don't bother me, and I already know that my ears are very ugly..." stuttered Chico, and his face darkened for a moment, and it almost seemed that he was going to pout. But he regained his composure right away and continued, "I don't mind that they eat my candies. I hope they eat them all and get a terrible stomach ache. I'll earn more money and buy a lot more."

And saying that, Chico went back to sitting on the stoop by the doorway, with his arms crossed and his back straightened up like a proud merchant, with big ears, waiting for his customers to arrive.

CHAPTER SIX

The cats' room was truly full of cats. Black, gray, brown, tiger-striped cats, cats with white paws, broken paws, some sickly, others with paunches; slender, flirtatious cats, prepubescent kittens, big tomcats full of scars from their fights with the other males. The window always remained open so that the animals could come and go when it suited them, but even so, the atmosphere was both fetid and overly sticky-sweet. Grandmother Barbara took care of the cats, and Amanda took care of Grandmother, Segundo, Chico, me, and the house.

Sometimes the felines didn't come alone, but returning from one of their nocturnal excursions, would bring home a friend. Grandmother Barbara, however, had picked up the majority of them on the street on the few occasions when she went out: generally, only twice a month, on the first and third Saturdays. Grandmother got all dressed up on those days; she washed and brushed her long, thin white hair very carefully, took out her dresses and spread them out around her room before deciding on one, and she polished her boots with all the buttons, which on her enormous feet seemed like military ware. And finally, when she was completely dressed up, she would put a cinnamon stick in a tiny, refined handkerchief, and she would put the handkerchief in her neckline.

"Am I OK?" she would then say. "Am I bundled up enough? Or will I be too warm?"

Amanda would run to the window; she would put her arm out to test the air, she gazed at the sky, but, because she was insecure and hesitant, she was never able to respond to Grandmother Barbara's questions adequately. Grandmother would grumble dissatisfied. She would take off her jacket and put it back on, walking around the room a few times, while Amanda became more and more nervous and as the intensity of the impending departure increased. And at last, neither before nor after, but at the right moment, as if an honorary gun-salute had sounded, Grandmother Barbara would finally open the door and slowly cast off from her room as if on a majestic transatlantic journey through distant seas.

Actually, she always went to the cemetery. I know because she brought me with her many times. She carried her cane in her left hand, and with her right she grabbed me by the neck, and it was like having a vulture clinging to my back. People looked at us a lot. They looked at us in the Neighborhood, where we were famous since we bought the boarding house. But they looked at us even more in the city, where we arrived by bus. I know my Grandmother dressed in a strange way, but then she seemed like a queen to me, and in the eyes of others I thought I saw fear or perhaps envy, never pity, curiosity, or disdain.

We used to go to the very small, old cemetery that, with the growth of the city, had remained almost in center of downtown. It was a pleasant place, most of all when it was sunny, and the trees drew a quivering puzzle of lights and shadows on the sandy ground. On those days, Grandmother seemed rejuvenate as soon as we entered through the wrought-iron gates. The noise of the cars stayed behind us, and the cemetery was a cool, vegetative bubble that smelled like freshly watered earth. Grandmother Barbara opened her enormous mouth and breathed the air noisily and greedily, as if she wanted to swallow it all in one gulp. Sometimes she would laugh; I didn't know why.

She would have me read the headstones and pay attention to the dates. Then she would squeeze my neck and say strange things:

"Look! 'In memory of my beloved wife, Matilde Morales Pérez, 1847-1901...' Take a good look at it... They are all dead, all of them, except for you and me... Don't ever forget it; never forget that you are living. Between the sea of shadows of the time that once was and the endless sea of time yet to come, you are living now, right now, a spark of light and chance in the midst of the void. A privilege. The truth is that I don't know why fools live. Or wretches. Why so much squandering of life by people. With all those people who don't even know they are alive. When I could make such good use of those years that others waste. It's not reasonable; it's not fair nor economical. If there is someone up above, he has done everything very poorly."

And she would let out a burst of laughter, and we would continue walking through the graves until the sun fell and the trees began to hiss that threatening moan that trees sing at night, and then the guard would come and tell us he was closing, and I could finally manage to tear my Grandmother away from the cemetery. Grandmother Barbara could never leave the places she liked.

It was on the return trip home when she would usually get hold of the cats. She grabbed the wildest and most fierce street animals by the scruff of the neck, and they would let her do it with an inexplicable tameness. Although it could have been because word of Grandmother Barbara's hospitality had already travelled among the Neighborhood cats, because on some occasions it even seemed that the cats would come out to meet us. Then, Grandmother would baptize each animal with the name of one of the deceased, Matilde Morales Pérez, Lucy Annabel Plympton, Rodrigo Ruiz Roel, names that she had gathered in the afternoon in the cemetery, taken from the worn headstones. Grandmother Barbara had a good memory, and she always called each cat by the correct name. And so, when she entered the room to give them food and change their water, she would always talk with them for a little while, with the ones that were there, because since they came and went, the population varied. She addressed the animals by name and with great respect, as if she were dealing with people. And some truly did seem human: Lucy Annabel, a lovely innocent kitten; Rodrigo, a grumpy, raspy cat; Matilda, a matronly cat with round hips.

If I'm telling all this, it is because something disturbing happened in the cats' room. It was the day after our encounter with Buga, and I had spent the entire morning covering the Neighborhood to see if I could find my father; that is, that mysterious man who was looking for me. But I didn't find him, and I felt so sad that I went into the cats' room. I did that once in a while; I slipped in without anyone seeing me because no one was ever there, except for Grandmother in the mornings. Once I overcame the stifling odor, which one would get used to in a few minutes, I felt safe and supported there.

That morning I must have fallen asleep because some voices startled me, and when I opened my eyes, the room was dark. I understood immediately that there was someone in the adjoining room, the one with the couch, the one Segundo used as a living room. A wood door crowned by a transom linked the two rooms, and the light and a man's voice slipped in through the small window.

"I'm telling you that we're going to have problems. He is looking for you, and I am sure he knows everything."

"But what the fuck is everything? Don't try to be smart, Portuguese." Segundo's voice was furious.

"You know what I'm referring to... I know it, too. And I'm not trying to be smart... for now."

"Don't threaten me, Portuguese, don't threaten me..."

On the other side of the door there was a short, tense silence.

"Fine. Let's not argue. We're partners, right?" Portuguese said in an appeasing tone.

More silence.

"I'm telling you the guy is a danger. He comes from inside."

"I know. And I'm sure Maximo sent him."

I pricked up my ears upon hearing my father's name. So the recent arrival was not him, but, yes, it was someone on his behalf. And Segundo seemed to be afraid of him.

"Maximo doesn't know anything either," said Segundo with a hesitant voice.

"He knows that you have the money."

Chairs dragging, a sharp blow, a sudden panting, and Segundo's whispering and outraged voice could be heard, "Do not repeat that again... Do not even think that again, you hear, Portuguese? If you say that again, I will slit your throat..."

Silence again, interrupted only by a few shallow gasps.

Shortly afterwards, Segundo spoke again in a calmer tone, "The money burned in the fire."

"Yes... in the fire."

"It was a tragedy."

"A damn tragedy..." grumbled Portuguese.

"And if my brother's wife died, it is not my fault."

So, my father had been married, I thought, surprised, and it was news that bothered me. But immediately it seemed as if a heavy drape inside my head had been drawn back, and the whole room was lit up by my discovery: that woman they were talking about, who died in the fire, had to be my mother. I felt a heatstroke in my face, my breath sizzling and sweet from the flames. My legs trembled, and I fell to the floor. I threw a chair, and I must have made considerable noise.

"What was that?" Portuguese was startled.

"Nothing. The cats' bullshit."

I heard a few steps, and the door opened. A triangle of blinding light ran along the floor until it reached me. I remained motionless where I was, still sitting on the tile floor, terrified and confused while Portuguese gazed at me coldly. He was the guy with the scarred mouth who I had seen in the hallway nights before.

"You were right ... It was the cats," the man finally said without breaking his stare.

"You see?" Segundo's voice was heard from the room. "The worst is that you don't believe me. Things in life are not going to go well for you that way, Portuguese."

"Yes, I believe you. The money was burned in the fire. You see? I believe you."

And before closing the door, he smiled, and his gold tooth flashed through the torn flesh of his mouth.

CHAPTER SEVEN

Everything changed when Airelai finally arrived. First her trunks arrived; there were so many heavy trunks with iron rivets on the corners and thick leather straps covering the locks. A couple of men from a moving company brought them, which was quite an event in the Neighborhood where no one who moved used that type of company because it was too expensive. I already said we had to be rich.

She appeared when they had already brought up almost all the bulky luggage. She was wearing a black felt beret adorned with a bright blue feather, a black leotard and a short, gauze skirt that was the same dazzling blue as the feather. All of her, from her flat, little patent leather shoes to the highest point of her hat, must have measured less than a meter. She came up to my chest, even though I was just a girl.

They opened the two rooms that had remained empty from the old boarding house, and they filled them with Airelai's luggage. They had to shift the furniture to one side, and there was hardly any space for anything else. The most extraordinary things began to emerge from the trunks: big swords and small daggers, Chinese folding screens made of rice paper, lacquer boxes that could be disassembled and reassembled like clockwork, tiny dresses embroidered with sequins, glass balls with lights inside, colored cubes, small folding tables, handkerchiefs and fans.

One of the trunks was padded and lined with dark red silk, and the little dwarf woman had her bed inside there, with linen sheets and a lace pillow. On the inside of the trunk's lid, Airelai had sewn some prints: some multicolored and disturbing drawings, which she later explained were Hindu gods, the photo of a whale jumping out of the water in the middle of the ocean; a beautiful green, mountain landscape with a stone house on the hillside; an old sepia-colored portrait of a very small woman up on a table dressed in a long dress; and lastly on the fifth and most fascinating print, an explosion of light on a dark background, like a sparkling ball of fire in the darkness. That was the Star, Airelai explained to me; it was a photo of the Star; I learned what it looked like by heart thanks to that image, and that is why, when I saw it later, I was able to recognize it.

Airelai brought magic. I mean that she and Segundo began to do a magic show in the club that was across from our house. Because that is what those doors were -- reddish, smoking doors that only opened at night were clubs. What a club was, that I did not know. But it was certainly not a place for girls.

The dwarf woman's arrival was an event. Even Grandmother Barbara seemed to be glad. She got up from bed to welcome her,

"It's about time you showed up," she blurted out as a greeting.

"They wouldn't let me bring my trunks across the border," Airelai apologized.

"You need to get to work as soon as possible"

"There's not such a hurry," Segundo complained.

"Sure there is, stupid," scolded Grandmother. "You're raising eyebrows with so much money... The police are already investigating; that's what Rita from the store said."

"That wasn't the police," Segundo protested, "It was..." he bit his lip, "Well, perhaps yes, perhaps you're right."

Grandmother Barbara looked at him with eagle eyes and with the same expression that a bird would gauge a worm, which it is going to swallow up within one second. Then her iron look dissolved; her heavy chin trembled; she seemed older. She sighed.

"You're not even a shadow of your brother."

She turned around, entered her rooms, and slammed the door. Segundo rocked from one foot to the other and looked at the dwarf woman.

"She's crazy. Now you see, crazier each day. But just to be clear, the one who gives the orders around here is me. You understand?" he said with a tinge of threat in his voice.

"Yes."

"And he will never return. He can't. He has many more years left. And when he returns..."

An airplane passed over us, and its boom ate the rest of Segundo's words. I saw the dwarf woman move her head and repeat, "Yes."

And then, I don't know why, the two turned and looked at me. I faked being absorbed in cracking hazelnuts in the doorjamb, which was my excuse for staying in the hallway. But Segundo grabbed the dwarf woman by the arm and took her, almost airborne, to the room with the couch, and I couldn't hear any more.

Some days later, Amanda, Chico, and I went to the club across the street to see the rehearsal for the magic act. It was in the morning, and when we pushed the door open, neither the smoke nor the reddish glow could be seen. Truthfully, the place turned out to be quite disappointing: it was a kind of large warehouse full of furniture. There were imitation leather armchairs, and the tables were all scratched up, and some of the armchairs had holes where their stuffing was escaping. On the floor there was wall-to-wall carpet covered with burns and spots, and the walls were so dirty that it was impossible to determine their color. In the corner there was a stage formed by a wooden platform and some green curtains with gold fringe that were filthy and ripped, like everything else. No window could be seen, and the only light came from some dusty bulbs that were hanging from the ceiling. It smelled sour and like stale tobacco. It was such a sad place it made your heart sink.

Airelai was dressed up in a full costume all embroidered with red and strawberry-colored sequins; she looked like a little flame burning atop the old wood of the stage. Segundo was wearing a silk robe that was big on him. He was folding the baggy sleeves over his elbows, and he stepped on the hem as he was walking.

"Damn it ... Amanda!"

"Yes..." Amanda stammered from the half-light.

"See if you can sew this..."

"Yes, yes, sorry, I'll do it later."

Segundo was in a dreadful mood. It was one o'clock in the afternoon, and he never got up so early. On top of that he didn't enjoy the magic tricks. He made silver triangles appear and disappear under hats, he made paper flower stems multiply, and he untied ropes in the air, never ceasing to grumble with a gloomy frown.

"Do you notice something strange? Did you see the tug with my left hand? Amanda!"

"No! No, it's OK; everything is very good, very good..."

Amanda was biting her nails, and Chico was sitting next to her with his head tilted to one side. Like every time he found himself with his father, Chico maintained a silent and lethargic demeanor as if he were drowsy, but he had his ears perked up and alert, like a rabbit's ears.

Segundo had brought us to the club to rehearse the show. Behind him, in a weightless, quiet flutter of sequins, Airelai arranged everything and handed him the equipment. I only watched her. She was so beautiful and everything else so ugly.

That's why I got worried when Segundo put her in a box, with her little hands on the sides and her feet at the bottom; the dwarf woman moved her hands and feet, which looked like small animals with a life of their own. Segundo began to drive the hefty, large blades with carved handles into the box; they hissed unbearably as they cut through the wood and appeared, sharp and clean for the most part, on the other side, but I feared they would come out stained with blood. And when the trunk seemed to be a pincushion already, and it was impossible for anything to fit inside without having been skewered, Airelai still remained smiling and intact. For me, that was the first indisputable proof of the dwarf woman's power.

Because she was the one who had magical powers, not Segundo. That's how Amanda and Chico and I understood it right away, and that's how Airelai explained it to us later herself.

"This works like ventriloquists. You know what they are? Have you seen them? They are those people who appear on stage with a dummy, and they talk and tell jokes, and they pretend the dummy has a voice. But I know that's not how it is; listen to me carefully. I know that it is the dummy who speaks instead of the ventriloquist, and then pretends that the ventriloquist is pretending that the dummy is talking. You understand? On stage I also pretend that the magician is the one who knows the tricks, but, in fact, it is I who keeps the secret, and who possesses the power of speech. Listen carefully , without me, they would be nothing."

CHAPTER EIGHT

Grandmother was leaving, and I was running toward home to say goodbye, when, as I was turning the corner, I collided with a man. It was like crashing into a wall. Two huge hands fell on my shoulders, and a gray face lowered itself until it was a few centimeters from mine.

"I'm sorry... " I muttered.

In my flustered state, I could only see a canvas of worn skin before me, a thick stony-faced, pock-marked skin. The skin stretched, and a row of yellow teeth appeared, and higher up I discovered two fixed, round eyes, like those of a shark.

"I'm sorry," I repeated, and I pulled away with my shoulders, trying to escape, but he held me tight.

"What a coincidence. What a coincidence," the guy said showing his teeth threateningly. Even though that was his way of laughing. "You. I was looking for you."

"No, not me. No, not me." I answered right away, squirming in his hands. It wasn't possible that this guy who was so awful could have been sent by my father.

"You're Tiger's daughter."

"No, not me. No, not me." I repeated with more certainty, relieved to confirm that I really did not know one iota about this Tiger guy.

"Of course it's you, Maximo's daughter. But hasn't anyone talked to you about your father?"

I pulled away and freed myself from his huge hands. I went running down the street, and I heard him laugh at my back, "No matter how much you run, I'll be waiting for you."

I arrived home breathless, just in time to see how a large taxi took Grandmother away to an unknown, far away destination. Grandmother Barbara had changed her gorgeous clothes for a dark gray tailored suit. Every five or six weeks, she put on that sad and boring suit, grabbed her leather bag and disappeared for a couple of days, and when she returned, she came back sick. She went to bed and ordered that the blinds be closed as if she were sleeping, and we all tiptoed around the house — everyone except Segundo, who on those occasions kicked the furniture, slammed doors, and seemed to be more agitated than ever.

The day that I collided with the man was the first time that Grandmother left, and I was frightened that Grandmother Barbara would be gone right when a threat was prowling around us. But that guy didn't want anything bad to come of us; I was sure of that. I told Airelai the whole story after Grandmother had left: about the man's words, his calloused hands, and harsh eyes.

"It had to happen," the dwarf woman murmured, and her small, slight face darkened.

She didn't say anything else, and the afternoon passed without anything memorable happening, though perhaps it passed with more silence, maybe with more sadness. But at night when Chico and I were sleeping, Airelai came into our room and woke us up, "Oh, little sleepyheads, open your eyes and get up... We're going to explore the world a little...."

Amanda was behind her, dressed in just a long t-shirt, with her skinny legs and bare feet as if the dwarf woman had just gotten her out of bed, too. Amanda appeared over Airelai's shoulders with her hair disheveled and embarrassed by an attack of nervous laughter. She looked like a girl, not a mother, and being Chico's mother, this was troubling and irritated me. But Chico put his arms out to her right away, smiling and dozy, and Amanda picked him up in the air, and squeezed him against her chest, and danced about with him throughout the whole room in the midst of big peals of laughter. And I did not have any warm, perfumed neck to grab onto. Baba.

"Come, come! Segundo went out, and Grandmother Barbara is not here... We're alone!" the dwarf woman urged, smiling.

They hadn't turned on any lights, I realized now. The house was dark and silent, and the glow of the full moon came through the wide open window. The world seemed enveloped in that silver air, so clean and so light. The sink in the corner, the closet, the door, even our hands, and the gleam of our teeth when laughing; everything looked more clear and more beautiful . Sweet and weightless, like the essence of good dreams. It truly seemed that we were still in bed and that we had done nothing but dream.

That is why we didn't bother to put our clothes on, and like Amanda, we followed the dwarf woman bare-footed in t-shirts because that way of dressing, or not dressing, was the most appropriate for a gem of a night like that one, a different kind of night -- one that seemed like it would never be vanquished by the sun -- the eternal night. And that way, we danced and jumped from room to room in line behind Airelai, and we went about opening all the windows we passed. And the silent, liquid moon came in with a torrent, drawing large rectangles of light on the floor and lapping our bare feet with its cold tongue.

"How beautiful the night is," said Airelai. "Nights of dark houses and empty kitchens, open balconies and the smell of recently watered geraniums ... The night belongs to women. And to children, until they become men and forget who they are."

And she opened the door to the cat room and let the animals follow us throughout the house, and they sharpened their nails on Segundo's couch.

It was June, and it was already beginning to get hot; the smell of early summer dawns came in through the windows. It was a warm, dry aroma, like pressed sheets or freshly fired clay. We went to Amanda's room, then to the dwarf woman's to rummage through her treasures, and then we ran or perhaps we flew to the kitchen, where we devoured spoonfuls of honey, that in the moonlight, was shining and black like melted jet.

"At night, things keep their own shadows, and that's why they're different during the day when all things are severed in two, and their shadows leave them, and everything loses a little of its essence," Airelai explained. "But, of course, since you two spend the nights sleeping like logs, you haven't realized that."

And the dwarf woman must have been right because that thick, black honey was the most delicious I had ever eaten; and also because everything was similar to what it usually was, but everything was different: the transparent colors, the furniture floating weightlessly in the twilight, the cool tiles caressing our feet. The house seemed to breathe around us like a kind, affectionate animal, and the air was light and frothy, as if the moonlight had been whisked until it became whipped cream.

We went into Grandmother Barbara's room, stumbling over each other, opening our eyes wide in order to notice all the details. The armchair was a furious guardian submerged in the shadows, and when the dwarf woman opened the drapes, it became a throne in the moonlight. And Grandmother Barbara's shadow seemed to rest in bed. We were all quiet; the cat, Manuela Fornoz Sanz, who had entered with us, lowered her head and went on tiptoes. Moving with the confidence of someone who knows the place, the dwarf woman opened the lower drawer of the dresser, and took out the square box of pine nut pastries. We each took one, and sitting in a semi-circle on the floor, we ate them at the same time, nibbling, as if it were a ritual. Beneath us, the world was turning.

Even without her being there, the room smelled like Grandmother, like incense and liniment. I looked at my father's photo; his face stood out in the twilight, strong and intense.

"That's Maximo, yes," murmured the dwarf woman, who was watching. "I was there when he had that photo taken."

I tried to feign disinterest because I didn't want them to find out that I was waiting for my father's imminent return.

"And the other portrait?"

"That is of Grandmother Barbara's husband. Your grandfather. He was a very good magician. I learned a lot from him," answered Airelai.

"He scares me," said Chico.

"It's because he's dead. Do you understand what I'm telling you? When they took the photo, he was already dead. He never consented to being photographed while he was alive. He used to say that photos steal one's soul."

Those dreadful blue eyes, the bloodless muscles of his face. Chico embraced his mother.

"He scares me," he repeated. And he curled up in Amanda's lap.

Twisted like he was, his light t-shirt had crept up to his mid back. I saw his white, smooth child's skin, the pointy bones of his spine, and those strange, round, dark marks. I leaned and looked more closely; they were small circles of wrinkled, darker skin. There were two or three; perhaps there were more underneath. They could have been burns. Scars.

"What do you have there?" I asked.

Chico gave a start, and covered his back with one fell swoop. And then, from his expression, I understood. I understood why he was so careful getting undressed, when I had thought it was his male modesty. I understood his terror of Segundo.

We remained silent for a long while, while the night kept flickering light all around. Amanda cradled Chico in her arms and mumbled a lullaby just for him. Now she didn't seem like a girl, but rather much older than she really was. Airelai got up with a sigh and approached the open window. I followed her. There below, next to the streetlight on the corner, leaning on the wall, was the man who I had run into that morning. He was smoking a cigarette, and he seemed to be waiting for something or someone with tireless patience.

"It had to happen," the dwarf woman repeated.

An airplane tore through the sky over our heads; it was like the sound of masses of stone rolling. Then, it began to dawn, and that eternal night, too, came to an end.

CHAPTER NINE

Airelai had a mark of the Caravacan cross drawn on the roof of her mouth. One day she showed it to us, and as she was so short she had to go up on the kitchen table so that Amanda could see it. It consisted of a whitish rim that went across her palate; it didn't prove to be too spectacular, but it was the mark of the Star.

"This shows that I have the gift."

Chico and I immediately examined each other's mouth to see if we were marked. But no.

"Don't be foolish. If you had it, you would know because this isn't the only sign," said the dwarf woman. "The most important is the power of the word. If a child has the gift, he speaks from his mother's womb. But if the mother speaks of this, if she reveals the prodigy, the infant is born with the mark but loses the gift."

We were awestruck. Even Amanda pursed her lips, frightened by the immeasurable consequences of talking.

"That's why you're like that, because you have that thing in your mouth?" asked Chico timidly.

"What do you mean like that?"

"Little like that."

Airelai puffed up her tiny chest and took a few steps from one side to another with a satisfied air, as if the boy had given her the greatest tribute.

"Let's say that I am ... special," she finally answered with a smile.

And then she told us about the Star.

Airelai talked a lot, for along with her, her trunks, her magic show gear, and her costumes embroidered with sparkles of light, the main thing that arrived were words: fascinating stories of distant worlds, extraordinary adventures, incomprehensible but surely important reflections. So when Chico and I didn't understand something, we learned the phrases by heart, convinced that life, with time, would end up conforming to Airelai's words and that would allow us to extract their meaning. Our dwarf woman knew everything. She looked very young - an elegant doll without a past —but she assured us that she was very old.

"I'm not a dwarf, but rather a Lilliputian, that is with dainty proportions; not abnormal or monstrous, just small," Airelai explained often. "We Lilliputians are life's miniatures, perfect models, and for that very reason, because of our perfection, we never age. We are never completely children, or elderly either. We are always exactly the same as we traverse existence, and in the end on any day, we die. Like everyone does. But we tend to live a long time because since we're small, death often forgets us."

Naturally, she was brilliant and beautiful with skin the color of just toasted bread, dark eyes, thick, straight hair so black it had bluish highlights. And a delicate, sweet voice, adorned here and there with hints of a foreign accent, which slipped into your ears like a cool breeze. With that light, hypnotizing voice, Airelai told us the following story that afternoon:

"I was born very far from here, toward the East on the other side of seas and mountains. Right when my parents were making love without thinking of me, a wandering star, which is the most powerful because they don't need to be stupidly attached to a fixed place in the firmament, passed above them, and behold my parents conceived me that instant, and I obtained my strength from the nearby fire of the Star. And at six months I spoke inside of my mother's womb, and I shouted, "I want to get out of here!" That was the obvious proof that I had the gift, not just for speaking but rather for saying that I wanted to get out, because everyone knows that no child wishes to abandon his mother's womb and, so alone and so naked, face the painful weight of the world."

"But I was not so alone because I had my gift. And that granted me the power of clairvoyance and understanding. Unlike the rest of humanity — people who are so absorbed and enclosed in their little existence that ahead, and behind, they only manage to see darkness. I knew where I came from and who would arrive behind me. I know that I occupy my place in the chain of life, like a miniscule lost drop, but also clothed in the waters of a torrential river. The Star, which is accustomed to the astral, superhumanly slow rhythm of the great heavenly bodies gave me that keen perception of the vast and the minute. I know that I am small, very small; but the rest are too, and they don't know it. That is my power, that of consciousness."

"When she heard me yell inside her womb, my mother was carried away with tremendous fright. My mother was very young then, and she had become an orphan while still a girl, so my Grandmother, her mother, didn't have time to pass on some basic, essential knowledge like knowing what you should do if your child begins to speak to you from inside. The fact is that my poor, frightened mother at first was quiet and did nothing, hoping to have heard wrong. But I was always very impatient and pig-headed, so I kept yelling that I wanted to get out. Until finally one afternoon my mother got ready carefully, elegantly, and wrapped her belly with a wool shawl to muffle my voice, and she went walking to the other end of town to consult the old wise woman. And the old wise woman told her:

'Woman, you have done the wrong thing in coming. You have revealed to me that your child yells inside you, and just for that, for talking too much, the infant could lose her gift: you should never have told anyone. You have an excuse, nevertheless, and that is that you didn't know, and that even without knowing, you have acted with considerable judgment and discretion, and you have only told me while looking for advice. So you deserve my help, and I'm going to do it, even though I don't know if we'll manage to compensate for this mistake. The first thing you must know is that, when one has incited an unfortunate destiny, the only way to avoid it is to exchange it for some other affliction. If you don't want your infant to lose her gift, she'll have to pay for it in some way. That is, she'll have to choose between the gift and pain. But I'm not the one to decide something so important for your child; not even you can do it. I remember that so many, many years ago, when I was still a girl, my Grandmother, who taught me all that I know, took me one day to visit a great stone and wood house on the outskirts of town. A couple of men—I don't know if they were relatives or servants—led us up the granite stairs and took us to the master bedroom. There, on an immense bed that they had reinforced with oak planks, an older woman—more or less my Grandmother's age—was lying down. She had her eyes closed and she was breathing painfully, but most notable was the colossal belly that she had – a volume of unreal dimensions that blew her nightgown up like a sail, and rested laterally on the bed. Her abdomen was so large that the old woman seemed like an appendage to it and not the contrary. Then my Grandmother told me,

"That woman with a colossal belly who you see here was my best friend at one time. We grew up together, and together we went to our first dances. She met a good, handsome boy right away, and she got married. A little later she became pregnant, and her happiness seemed so complete that it was almost frightening. But at six months pregnant, the baby began speaking to her from inside the womb. It was a male and he would say sweet, pretty things. My friend knew that she shouldn't tell anyone about the prodigy, but at that time she found herself blinded by the mindless intoxication of power that happiness and love produce. So she told her husband, and then, scared about what she had done, she asked for help from her close women friends who explained to her that if her son wanted to keep his gift, he would have to pay for it with unhappiness and misery. Their advice didn't mislead her, but, as you'll see later, it was incomplete. The fact is that my friend thought about it a lot – nights without sleeping and days of weeping. And in the end she decided that her son could not lose his gift even though the price was high. So one early morning she went out on the patio and under the dim light of the stars, and in the name of her son she accepted the necessary afflictions provided that he would keep the gift. Well then, that was the worst thing she could have done. The boy screamed upon hearing her, and he didn't stop screaming inside her womb for several days. But the most dreadful was that weeks passed and her due date arrived, and the infant didn't come out; he refused to live a life of misery that others had chosen for him. One week late came to an end, then a month, the first year, the second, the third year passed; the boy wasn't born, but he grew inside his mother at the same pace as if he had been growing outside. Soon the weight and the volume were so tremendous that my poor friend could no longer be upright, and she became bedridden for life. And there, in bed, the boy continued developing and finally he stopped being a boy and became a real man. And judging by the size of her belly, he must have been a tall, strong boy, and now he must be a considerably fat fifty-something. Many years ago my friend lost consciousness completely; she only lives to feed herself, something that she has to do for several hours a day, and the rest of the time she generally dozes."

'That's how my Grandmother told it,' said the old wise woman. And the two of us went on contemplating the mountain of trembling flesh in the half-light; we could hear a distant, weak man's voice that exclaimed, "I don't want to leave," between damp echoes, reverberations in her belly's dome, and splashing. If I tell you all this, woman, it's so that you will understand that we can't make decisions for others in any way. That it's not fair at all to impose a destiny that we have chosen on others, even though we believe that we are doing it for their well-being.'

"That's how the old wise woman told it," said the dwarf woman, "and having learned her lesson, my mother returned home. And that same night she went out onto the patio, in the dim light of the stars, and she told me that I had to choose between suffering and the gift. I rebelled and kicked about inside my mother's womb because it seemed unfair to have to assume responsibility for such a decision before even being born. But finally I chose, I preferred the gift, because I prefer knowledge, even with misery, to a foolish happiness without consciousness."

"Well then, I was so worried during the last months of my gestation, that I spent so much energy on deciding on the best option, and I neglected the final touches of my anatomy, and so it happened that when I was born, I was very small, and soon one could see that I must have been missing an essential part of the growing mechanism, because time passed, and I continued to be diminutive, until my condition as a Lilliputian became evident. Then I discovered that this type of mishap is quite common. I'm trying to say that many pregnant women touched by the gift talk too much; and their children, upset by having to live through such tremendous conflicts while still in the maternal womb, tend to neglect their own formation or, out of sheer anxiety and bewilderment, they confuse the assembly pieces. And so many are born with six fingers on each hand, with their feet twisted, or with a cleft lip. So when you meet those peculiar beings with a sad appearance out in the world, hunchbacked, or blind, or knock-kneed men and women, or those as ugly as a devil and crippled and cross-eyed, don't believe that they are inferior for that, or deserving of pity, because they are probably that way because they possess the gift."

"As far as I'm concerned, I have never regretted my decision, even though my life has been difficult, and I have always had to live with some misery. But also, thanks to the gift, my life is intense. And I know, besides, that my Star, which is a wandering star — one that the men of science call a comet, will return one day. You have seen the photo of my comet, of my Star, because I have sewn it in the top of my trunk: that mass of light, that lovely sparking, that power. One night that is not so distant now, it will return to cross the sky above me, and that night, I know, my suffering will have ended, and all my wishes will become reality. I know it will happen like that; it will happen."

This is how Airelai spoke when she told us about the Star, leaving Chico, Amanda, and me gaping. Night had fallen over her words, and we remained quiet for a few minutes in the twilight following the story.

Then Amanda asked, "And if you say that you always have to endure some pain, what misery plagues you now?" Because the dwarf woman seemed strong, free, and happy to us.

Airelai sighed, "Well now ... I am suffering a lot now," she said blushing, "Although you might not notice, I'm suffering a lot from love."

CHAPTER TEN

Since the guy with the shark's smile began to watch the house, Segundo had disappeared. He didn't say where he was going, or even that he was going to leave; he simply left the boarding house one afternoon and still has not returned. In the beginning, Amanda was more pale than ever, and she couldn't get to sleep at night waiting for her husband's return.

"I don't want him to catch me sleeping," she would remark to Grandmother at times.

"He was always a complete good for nothing," Grandmother Barbara would answer.

As the days passed, Amanda seemed to calm down, and at times she could be heard humming something while she prepared food or cleaned the house. Though sometimes she would abruptly stop her soft melody and startled, she would lift her hand toward her face, with that gesture that was so her, so undefined, as if she were going to cover her mouth and changed her mind halfway, as if she were going to bite her nails, and she had lost her fingers on the journey.

And her entire life was depicted in that hand dangling limply in the air.

"I can't believe he left," she murmured, distressed at those times. "He'll come back. I know it. He will never leave me."

We lived with our ears pricked up, waiting to hear his steps at any moment. We talked, we played, we ate, and we slept with that impending presence, and we did everything in a hurry in order to finish before he came back, even if the activity in question was totally innocent. But Segundo's return was a line, a border, and the longer it took, the more imposing the moment of his homecoming seemed—charged with more meaning and threat.

"It's possible that he will never come back again," the dwarf woman said as she fanned herself with a piece of cardboard.

It was time for an afternoon nap, and the air was still and muggy.

"I cannot believe it," answered Amanda.

"Why?"

"It's not my luck. I mean, I have very bad luck."

"But suppose that has changed," said Airelai. "Now you have my strength. You three have my fortune. When my Star arrives, all your wishes will come true. And I want you three to be happy: you, Amanda; and you; and Chico, too. So my luck is now your luck."

Amanda sighed, "You are the one who is so good, Airelai. But he will come back."

I stretched out on my back on the floor, enjoying the temporary coolness of the tiles. Above me was the room's stagnant, warm air; and above that the seared roof; and above that an almost white sky scorched by an unbearable sun; and above that the ever black firmament that surrounds us, like I had seen on a TV program. And there, in the immensity of that eternal night, our Star was moving forward toward us, steady and blind, willing to grant us everything.

"Why haven't you broken away? Why haven't you left them?" the dwarf woman asked.

Amanda took a long time answering. She was seated on a chair, dressed in a t-shirt with old jeans cut off at her mid thigh. From time to time, she dipped a napkin in the pitcher of water that was on the table (we had just finished eating a little while ago), and she moistened her neckline and nape of her neck. The pitcher had had ice in it, but it had already melted. We were all moving slowly, and we were speaking slowly, and we were thinking slowly, as if moving, speaking, thinking, or breathing were dangerous; that is, as if the heat were killing us. And maybe it was. Chico wanted to curl up in Amanda's arms, but she felt smothered and pushed him away gently. Then, like me, the boy sprawled out on the floor, on top of the tiles, and he started to doze while holding onto one of his mother's ankles with his hand. Grandmother must have been taking an afternoon nap also in the stifling half-light of her rooms; she took sleeping pills. And, around us, the earth was burning.

"But, how could I leave?' That's impossible," Amanda answered finally.

"When you came here, alone, to pick up the girl..."

"They had kept the boy so that I wouldn't leave. Plus, where would I go? Segundo would find me. And he would kill me."

"Come on—you're not the only woman in a bad marriage in the world. Others have done it."

"Not me. I know. Not me."

"Plus you're a skilled girl; you have worked as a secretary; you know how to type... You don't need them for anything. Look for a job. Take the boy and go."

Amanda took a long time to answer again. She stared into space; you could see that she was forcing herself to imagine how her life could be without Segundo, without his brutality, without his rough, cruel hands. Drops of water and sweat shone on her neckline, and her wet hair stuck to her soft, round cheeks. A botfly was piercing the half-light above my head; it charged the thick, heavy air over and over again, and seemed to like the sound of the shadows as it tore through them. If Amanda left, she would take the boy. Just the boy. Baba.

Amanda sighed and shook her head hopelessly, giving in to defeat, "It's not my luck. My mother didn't want me to marry Segundo. But he was very handsome. I got married, and it all ended. Before, I was someone else, but I made a mistake, and there is no solution. I can't escape from him. That's how life is. It's over, Airelai."

Amanda was speaking with her gaze low, and an odd trembling softened her mouth and chin, as if they were rebelling against her, and even trying to escape from her face, and she lacked enough strength to hold her chin and mouth in place. Then I remembered another shaking and contrite chin like that, desperate in its attempts to escape from under the nose of its owner. Chico and I had seen it the afternoon before across the street from the house, at the door of the club, where, before Segundo disappeared, he and Airelai used to perform as magicians. It was Buga's, the cocky gang banger's, chin. But this time, when Chico and I saw him, he seemed considerably meek, and he was alone.

"I came to talk to Portuguese," Buga had gasped to the thug who opened the door for him and who left him waiting on the street.

When we saw Buga arrive, Chico and I hid in the shadows of our stoop. But the kid didn't pay the least attention to us; in fact, he seemed absorbed in something internal, and he was barely looking where he was going. With his chin trembling and his thick eyelids squinting over his slanted eyes.

"I told you not to come here. What the hell do you want..." grunted Portuguese, popping out of the door suddenly.

Buga's body shook under the man's voice. He leaned forward and whispered something that we didn't hear. Portuguese screwed up his torn mouth sarcastically, "And why would I do that for you? You're worthless. You're useless to me."

At that moment, the man with the shark's smile, who I had collided with a few weeks before, appeared next to Portuguese in the doorway. His presence was an unpleasant surprise to Chico and me— it had been a few days that we hadn't seen him, and we were beginning to think he had left. The Shark grabbed Portuguese's shoulders jovially and smiled with his gruesome mouth.

"What's happening?" he said, and there was something in his tone that changed those two innocent words into something brutal.

Buga leaned even closer to them and whispered again. We didn't hear him, but we saw his back, tensed forward and leaning down, too, in a gesture that was both eager and imploring at the same time. Portuguese changed his expression with distaste and pushed the kid away with a shove that almost threw him to the ground.

"Die," he said bored, without any enthusiasm, before going back inside the club.

"And don't come back," the Shark added, and it was clear that it was not just a piece of advice.

Buga stayed for a while gazing at the closed door, and then he turned around, and we could see his face: as white as a ghost. He stopped the trembling of his chin with his hand, and squeezed his lashless eyelids closed for a few moments. Then he opened his eyes, took a deep breath, puffed out his chest, and cast off walking down the street. In the last seconds, he had grown taller and more bold; he almost seemed like the Buga we always knew, if it were not for the wretched trembling of his chin.

Then Chico and I told Grandmother all about it. Not about Buga, but rather that we had seen Portuguese and the Shark, close and very friendly with each other at the magician's club.

"He was always a complete good for nothing," sighed Grandmother Barbara.

And she went to bed.

CHAPTER ELEVEN

We didn't have money. Earlier we were rich, but Segundo still hadn't surfaced, and we didn't have money. Grandmother had sold or pawned a gold watch and some large, heavy forks with an ornate arabesque pattern that looked like tridents. That's what Airelai, who knew everything, told me. But even so, we didn't have money. Some days, there was scarcely enough to eat, and Amanda prepared bread and spicy sausage for us and laughed a lot because, on one hand, she was worried about the financial situation, but on the other, she was beginning to think that Segundo would not return, and that emotional contradiction made her quite nervous and slightly crazy.

Then, Airelai said one day that it was OK, and that she was going to take matters into her own hands. She began to go out every night, cloaked in a mauve veil and in her mystery. She didn't return until very early in the morning; she took silent, weightless steps like a mouse and got into her trunk bed to sleep all day. I supposed that she was acting that way because of her magic, and that the reason she left home every night was to conjure spells in the moonlight. Because

Airelai always came back with money, little piles of wrinkled bills that she left on the table in the room with the couch before going to bed, and it seemed impossible to me that someone could find all that money during the dark nights if it weren't through some hex. In the morning, upon getting up, Chico and I would run to the table to see if the same miracle would repeat itself, and it was like every day was Christmas. I scrutinized the bills trying to find something special about them because I had never had the chance to see enchanted money before. But they looked like any other bills; some were even well worn and dirty, with their edges torn or things written in ink: ridiculous words, women's names, telephone numbers.

Then, Grandmother would arrive and pick up the little mountain of bills eagerly; she straightened, counted, and folded them. Then she would yell for Amanda, hand over some bills to her regally and order her to take care of the day's matters with the tone of an admiral: to pay for this or that, to buy port for her, to get chow for the cats, most of whom had left after not having food during the hard, hungry weeks of poverty, to the extent that only four felines had held out to the end: Zoilo Santana de Olla, Inés García Meneses, Tomasa López López, and Dolores Rubio González, to whom the grateful Grandmother had decided to bestow the title of duke and duchesses. Now, with the reappearance of the food dishes, the cats were returning little by little.

We had money, and Segundo was not there, so we were living with the best of both worlds so to speak. But we missed Airelai. Now we barely saw her, devoted as she was to her night-time spells and her restorative dreams during the day, and without the dwarf woman, without her ideas, without her stories, without her words, life was much less fun. So Chico and I spent our days overwhelmed by the weight of the summer, alone and bored. So bored that I began to allow myself to wander further and further: exploratory trips within the confines of the dusty Neighborhood. I wanted the boy to come with me, but he refused. Boredom didn't matter to Chico — what's more, he even seemed to enjoy it. Sitting on the stoop by the doorway, his little pale face gleamed with sweat. He was satisfied just to see the hours pass so still and calm. Playing with trading cards, making two cockroaches fight, or eating a mouthful of sausage were wonderful pleasures for him. Chico believed that dead calm was the best possible way to live because when nothing happens, there is no pain.

But I didn't think that way. I had hopes and desires; I was waiting; I was waiting for my father's arrival, or at least for the Star's arrival, which would herald our imminent happiness. And like anyone who awaits the beginning of a better life, I impatient lived the present time in great discomfort. I wanted to kill the hours—I wanted to kill time so that the future would arrive as soon as possible. But the summer was long and tedious.

For that reason, with my zeal to end the never ending afternoons, I began to explore the Neighborhood beyond the permissible area. We residents of the Neighborhood had our streets, our areas, the place in which, if we respected the rules, we could live in safety more or less. But if we broke those invisible, unspoken boundaries and we crossed into other territories, with other bosses, other gangs, other corners, other Bugas, then we could never be sure of the ground on which we stood or of the sky above. Everything was relative to the limits of the Neighborhood.

Nevertheless I began to come and go freely everywhere, and the summer and the heat helped me; the sun emptied the streets and blurred its surroundings with a blinding fog. I covered the north of the Neighborhood, which stretched toward the affluent part of the city, and I discovered the church with the ornate altar that reminded me of my Grandmother. I crossed to the East, and the Neighborhood was bordered by an area of factories with many men and women dressed in blue coveralls, and with police dogs sniffing the high barbed wire fences. I reached the edge on the West, and little by little, the Neighborhood gave way to dried out orchards and workers' housing that was partially in ruins in fields of barren earth consumed by thistles. And I went to the South last, and there I found more barbed-wire and police dogs because the Neighborhood bordered the airport, and they had gated the facilities to protect them. Even though, to tell the truth, it wasn't the airport that seemed fenced in, but rather the whole Neighborhood seemed to be locked inside a cage. Above all because it was here, in the South, where Casas Chicas was located.

To go South, first you would come across Violet Street, which wasn't violet during the day, nor was it noteworthy. I crossed it several times during daylight hours, (the ban was only in effect at night) and it was just a street like any other. It was wide and short with big, low windows that were always locked up. Then after crossing this street, the Neighborhood's asphalt immediately ended, and it became more and more gravelly. After walking just a little, you arrived at the dumps, some hills of rubble and trash where some dog, elderly person, or child was always rummaging. And crossing the dumps with their stench of rot, you came to the top of a small, steep slope, and you could gaze at Casas Chicas at your feet: it was a sea of overheating shacks, with tin and asbestos roofs, cardboard doors, Tetra-Pak carton walls. All of that within clouds of dust, rusted out car frames, skeletons of washers and refrigerators, half burned couches, nauseating grit, a triumphant parade of cockroaches and a sparkling sown field of broken glass. The shacks were squeezed against each other in the boiling hollow, with their backs to the airport's fences. Women's screams, children's cries, and the wary barks of starving dogs rose from the suffocating motley colors of the shanty town.

I had dared to go to Casas Chicas for the second time, and I was fascinated, observing the disturbing landscape from the top of the steep slope. I suddenly noticed a shadow that was not my own at my feet. I tried to turn around, but I didn't have time; a huge hand fell on me, and someone grabbed me like one grabs a cat by the scruff of the neck. A dark profile of a man who I could barely see neared my right ear.

"What a surprise... Look who's here."

The voice was familiar, but I was so terrified that I could not identify it.

"So you've come. I will have to do you the honors of receiving you. Let's go to my house."

Without releasing my neck, the man pushed me and made me descend the clearing in front of him. In the hollow, the heat was unbearable, and the sun seemed to roast even more; the dust came up above your ankles, and stuck to your sweaty legs. We walked for a while between the shacks, and barely anyone looked at us until, with a twist of his wrist, the man made me enter one of the houses through a small door. The inside was so dark that at first I couldn't see anything. Little by little the world around me began to materialize: the walls, formed by dozens of skim milk cartons; the floor, made of tamped earth was clean and well swept; a Formica table; a big bed with wood legs; a kitchen pantry; a butane burner; a TV and VCR. In the corner, so still that she was the last thing I saw, was an extremely skinny woman of some indeterminate age with a baby in her arms. She didn't look at me but rather at the man who had come with me, and she did it with petrified eyes, like a dog waiting to be punished. I noticed that my neck was now free, and I turned around. Smiling fiercely behind me was that man with the triangular mouth – Portuguese.

"Well, you'll want to drink something, right? You're my guest," he said sardonically.

And he turned toward the woman and barked something in a language that I didn't understand. Without letting go of the child, the woman strived to obey. She took out a Coke, a glass, poured the drink, and gave it to me. I sipped a little. It was as warm as soup.

"Good. You've had something to drink. You know my house. Now we've become friends. So now you can answer everything I ask you," said Portuguese.

I hurried to nod my head.

"Good. Where is the money?"

"What... what money, sir?" I stammered.

Portuguese's tooth flashed in his torn mouth. He grabbed me by the arms and lifted me up.

"Tiger's money... The money that Segundo had. Where is it?" he roared terrifyingly.

"I don't know; I don't know anything," I almost cried, "When Segundo went away, we were left without money... And now Airelai brings us cash at night..."

The man let me down to the ground with contempt.

"Yeah, I already know where the dwarf woman gets her cash ... But you won't trick me, not you, not her, not your Grandmother. I know that Segundo didn't take it because when they warned him, he fled without being able to go home. And he hasn't returned. So, from now on, you are going to look for me. You understand?"

I nodded again even though I didn't understand anything. Portuguese towered over me, "You are going to be my eyes, my hands, and my feet. You are going to search the whole house, you get it? Without anyone seeing you. The drawers, closets, under the beds, under loose tiles, in your Grandmother's room, in the kitchen. The whole house! You understand?"

I nodded again, and my submission seemed to calm him a little. The skeletal woman was still in the back of the room, stuck to the wall, motionless with the boy in her arms. The kid, who had to be between one and two years old, was playing with his mother's straight, dirty hair, and at a certain moment, he pulled it away from her face, and even though the woman hurried to cover it with her long hair again, I noticed that she was missing her right ear, and in its place there was only a jagged pink scar.

"I want that money. A lot of money. A suitcase full. Look for it. And look good. I'll give you a week. We'll see each other in seven days," said Portuguese softly as I played with my half empty glass of coke. "And don't think you can get away from me because you can't."

He closed his huge hand around the glass and without moving a single muscle in his face and without making any apparent effort at all, he made the glass shatter in a thousand pieces. He shook his hand, and two drops of blood fell to the ground.

"Next time," he warned, "it won't be my blood."

CHAPTER TWELVE

Grandmother was restless. She was tying and untying the knot on her purple blouse. She was arranging and rearranging the couch cushions over and over, because now that it was summer, she didn't stay in bed, but rather in the armchair strategically placed between the door and the balcony in order to catch a bit of breeze in that heavy, exhausting air. Grandmother Barbara sighed from time to time, and she sounded like an elephant trumpeting. It was a show of force.

"Doesn't it seem odd to you that death days don't exist?" she said suddenly. "We insist on celebrating the day of our birth, but we totally ignore the most important date of our lives, which is the day we die. And, nevertheless, that date comes and goes every year; we pass over that critical day completely blind and ignorant; even worse we get bored; we get irritated; we waste time without knowing that the same day, twenty years later, or five, or one, we would give anything just to make it to the next dawn..."

I was quiet; I already knew that she didn't want my response. Grandmother's big, spotted hands moved here and there in the air like tired birds who had lost their way and fallen off course. She was in a bad mood; she was surly and irritable, but this time — it was odd — I didn't feel intimidated. It was the first time that I saw her as old, instead of just massive and superhuman.

"Why are you doing this to me?" she exclaimed, hurt and complaining.

"Doing what?" I was startled.

But I immediately realized that this question was not directed at me either. Grandmother Barbara did that a lot; she talked to the corners and to the shadows. So I calmed down and continued drawing. I was painting a bright green sea, and a boat, and a seagull on paper. Then, Grandmother turned toward me and grabbed my hand.

"Look – what a hand. Look – such skin," she said in a dreamy, admiring tone, "Soft like my silk blouse. Firm and fresh. It is a pleasure to touch your hand. And to gaze at you. You're so brand new. So full of life that you're radiating in every direction. We elderly are so consumed by death that all those near us become tarnished with darkness. Perhaps you have noticed? No, not you. You're still too young a girl to notice.

She became quiet and let out another of her furious sighs.

"You children smell like vanilla. Even that disaster, that poor Chico, must smell that way. It's a warm, sweet little smell. I remember it well from when I held my children as babies. Segundo and Maximo. You bury your nose in them and breathe life's perfume. It's strange, but I can't remember the last time I smelled them like that. Those are other crucial dates that we miss as they pass by us. It is odd that you live those moments that are so important stupidly, without appreciating their magnitude. The last time that I smelled the last of my babies. The last time that I ran down the street for no reason, just for the pleasure of running. The last time that I went swimming out to the rocks in the sea. The last time that a man kissed me.

I abandoned my drawing because the conversation was becoming interesting.

"Was .... it grandfather?" I ventured, pointing at the man in the photo.

Grandmother looked at him, and she shrugged her shoulders.

"No. No. But that doesn't matter."

It was eleven in the morning, but the room was becoming dark as if night were falling. And the heavy, stifling, suffocating air entered the room with the shadows. Grandmother Barbara went back to untying the knot on her blouse, and then she let her hands fall on her knees, exhausted by the stifling heat.

"Promise me that you'll remember me. And that you will say my name out loud once in a while, like I say my cats' names, the names of those people who once lived and today have no one to mention them but me. Promise me that."

"Yes, but when do I have to do that?"

"When I die."

"But when you die, Grandmother, isn't the world going to end?"

"Of course it will end. But you will invent a new world for yourself."

It was a relief to know that. In that precise moment, the sky burst above our heads. First I thought it was an airplane, but then I realized that it had to be thunder.

"Finally! This heat was impossible," groaned Grandmother Barbara, standing up and heading toward the balcony.

I followed her and for a few minutes we did nothing other than gaze at the sky, which was black and swollen, and so low that it seemed that we could touch it with our hands. Lightening blazed a couple of times, and in those two moments I thought I would die, or I thought I would go blind at the very least, but with a unique blindness, the blindness of one who sees too much. Because, when the bolts struck, the street became lurid like the streets in bad dreams, and the sky was unmasked, and its true nature was revealed -- it was a great stony wall about to crumble and crush us. If the world is truly this way, if this is reality, I told myself, I prefer not to see and not to know.

In that moment dense, warm drops began to fall on us -- drops that burst deliberately and felt like fingers touching our skin lightly. We lifted our heads toward the black clouds, and the water caressed our faces. Grandmother opened her mouth, like she did sometimes on our visits to the cemetery, but this time it wasn't to swallow the afternoon air, but rather the rain. And the aroma of wet earth rose from the street as intoxicatingly as a drug.

Grandmother Barbara did not breathe, but rather she snorted like a large, powerful animal: a water buffalo, I remember thinking. She extended her arms out in the air and let herself get drenched by the sheets of rain. Her blouse stuck to her broad chest and her bony shoulders, and a trickle of drops fell from her prominent nose.

"Storms clean the air," she snorted to herself. "And the storm's rain cleans away the bad memories."

She began to rub her wet, bare forearms gently as if she were caressing herself, or perhaps as if she were caressing the drops that were on her skin. She squinted her eyes.

"The last time that I got soaked in the rain of the last summer ... Who knows? Maybe this is it," she said slowly.

We remained quiet for a few moments under the deafening drum roll of the water.

"Stormy rain like then. Like before. Do you remember him?"

"Who?" I stammered, while livid flashes were crossing above my head.

But I immediately realized that Grandmother Barbara was talking to herself again.

"His blue eyes ... were so beautiful. And not like in the photo. So full of life. It wasn't the sex. Of course not. Or not just that. It was knowing that he was my other half, and that there was nothing more that I required: not water, not shelter, not even breathing. On those afternoons when I desired him with such urgency and such feeling, ugliness did not exist, nor did age, nor did fear.

The thunder with its jagged edges shot through the sky sharply and rolled into a horrific roar, and it sometimes overshadowed Grandmother Barbara's words. But I listened to her so intently that I believe I heard everything. Even if I didn't understand.

"I still remember his skin. It was warm and soft, completely attached to mine. His young body, my young body. And our sweat mixing. Above all, I remember an emotion: feeling alive. Golden shadows from a lamp with a shade. A winter afternoon and the blue on the other side of the window. A cushion on the floor. I was always bad, except with him. I was always large and clumsy, except with him. I was always selfish, except with him."

Grandmother Barbara put out her arms again; I saw her wrinkled skin with its large age spots that the water had darkened. The storm was beginning to die down.

"Those who have not known love are so unfortunate. That type of love—that abyss into which one throws herself happily. Those who have never felt, even if for an instant, that she and her partner are the only two humans who have lived on this planet are so unfortunate. And those who have indeed felt it at one time are so unfortunate as well. Because they have lived it, and they have lost it. I was never so beautiful nor as intelligent as I was with him. Since then, to live has been to decline. Now, even though I am scarcely myself anymore and I forget everything, with all my misery, I am still unable to forget that agony of desire and of the flesh."

It thundered very far away now—a ridiculous little sound, like a cough from the sky. It was raining apathetically, a light sprinkle. Grandmother Barbara supported herself on the balcony's railing with both hands, and she leaned her sharp profile forward. She no longer seemed like a buffalo, but rather a dark bird, a wet, powerful young eagle about to spread her wings. But just when I hoped that she would fly away, the bird let go of the railing; she turned toward me and sighed. And then I could see that she was in fact just an elderly woman. My grandmother.

CHAPTER THIRTEEN

The dwarf woman had been a goddess, but she was no longer one. Because one can be a god and then stop being one, just as one can be in grace and later fall from it. There is nothing sure in this world; at any moment you can hear the bells toll for you, and you can lose all that you did not even know you had. That is what Airelai would say. And so one day, the dwarf woman told us about her divine past.

"I was born in the East, as you know well. Where the sun is born. In a world of great, tall mountains and very narrow trails where goats suffer from vertigo. It is a very ancient world; when I was little, progress had not even begun. The valleys were full of temples. Temples carved of wood or chiseled in stone. With broad lintels and very dark courtyards. There are many gods in those valleys. More gods than people. And almost all the gods are the usual type—that is, invisible; or most often, they have a stone statue or a painting to represent them. But there are three living gods, one in each of the three largest valleys of my land, and the most important of the three is the katami, and that was me.

"I was very beautiful as a girl. I don't want to sin for immodesty, but I am still lovely. As a girl I attracted attention; in my land there was no other child like me. I had just turned five years old when the katami who came before me bled her first drops of blood and lost her divinity. The priests came running out of the temple to look for a new goddess, mounted on donkeys on the narrow trails, and word of my existence reached them immediately because my beauty was such that the peasants mentioned it. So the priests arrived at my house shortly— first one, then another, and later the third who was the oldest and was completely bald. They began to look me over and inspect me from head to foot again because besides beautiful, the katami had to be free of defects. So they confirmed that I could see well, that I heard marvelously, that I had ten little fingers with ten little pink nails on my hands and feet. That my skin was all one color without freckles or spots, that I seemed healthy, and that my intelligence was above average. I was only a little diminished in size for my age, but after great deliberation, the priests decided that being petite was not truly an imperfection. They spoke with my mother, and my mother cried, and I cried, and they put me up on the donkey, and we left.

"I can assure you two that a goddess' work is extremely unrewarding. I used to dress beautifully, of course, with rustling crepe, stunning silks, and muslin as delicate and transparent as dragonfly wings; all were in shades that ranged from maroon to saffron because red is the katami's color. And then there was the gold, pounds of gold adorning my body – in rings that danced on my fingers that I had to tie with tiny pieces of twine, very heavy pendant earrings that pained my ears, bangle bracelets and anklets with bells that jingled with each movement, and belts, nose chains, and crosses. And there was gold in the complex hairdo that took several hours to re-do every day: with tiny hollow animal figurines that were strung in my hair. The katami's temple is a dark house, but my entire body shimmered of gold in the shadows.

"Everyday I woke up very early, and for several hours the priestesses dressed me and got me ready. Then I ate a healthy, boring meal for breakfast, and they began the teachings and liturgy, studies and rituals that lasted all day long. They treated me well; they always tried to please me, and they allowed my many whims (exotic birds, mechanical dolls brought from China, trained parrots), still I felt very unfortunate. In seven years I never left the temple, an old palace that lacked windows to the exterior and that only opened through a corridor onto a dismal courtyard, and I didn't have friends my age, and I never saw my family again. Or, more accurately, I only saw them below, in the courtyard, like the rest of the faithful, without being able to speak with them. I knew well that the sadness of my life as a goddess was a part of my destiny, and it was the painful dues I had to pay to keep my grace. Sometimes I looked at the miraculous Caravacan cross in my mouth with a polished brass tray (there were no mirrors in the katami's temple so that the goddesses would not be overwhelmed by the splendor of their own reflection), and I felt proud to have chosen knowledge despite the suffering. I never told the priests anything about my grace because I knew that gifts that they did not control would disturb them. Gods are always very distrustful regarding their powers, and the priests who serve them are even more so.

"From those resplendent and dark years, I remember the stories they told me, and above all, the teachings of the High Master, who was that old, bald priest. He came two or three times a week, and I felt happy listening to him. He talked to me about the visible world and the invisible, and of the essential instability of things, that is of how everything and everyone inevitably run toward destruction. He told me about the other gods, so that as a katami, I would know the tribe well. There were gods of all kinds, he told me: irate gods and benevolent gods, agricultural and war gods, fertility and death gods. But they were all speaking gods; we related to them with words, and they created worlds with the word. And so, in the beginning the majority of the deities had the Word, and then the Word became writing because writing is Law, and the gods always had the ambition of giving order to the world. For that reason all religions possess sacred books, and that is why there were cases like Woden or Odin, the god of the North and of ice, who hung himself on a tree and fasted, and tormented himself for a long time, while it rained and snowed on him, and the wind gnawed his blue, numb flesh until finally his penitence was rewarded, and he achieved mastery in the art of runes, which is the magical power of the written word.

"While the High Master was explaining all this to me, I was educating myself, and I learned to read and write. And not only in my everyday language, the language of food, drink, war, and love, but also in the essential language, the language of the substance of things, which is the one used in spells. I kept growing in wisdom but not in size. Years passed, and I continued to be as small as I was when I entered. And when I began to see the worry reflected in the priests' and priestess' eyes, I got up at night and cut a tiny piece from the hem of my robes stealthily so that they would believe that they were short on me because I had grown. That strategy calmed them for some months, but then they must have suspected something because they began to take my clothes at night and hide them in a large chest with two locks.

"In the end the situation became truly unbearable because I had turned twelve years old and not only had I not yet bled, like the rest of the katamis had done already at that age (in my land women mature early), but on top of that, my appearance continued to be exactly the same as the day when I entered the temple. The priests were horrified; they had chosen a defective katami, and there was no record of such a sacrilege in the entire goddess' millennia-long history. They didn't know what to do with me; they feared that I would never come to menstruate, and they were right because the flowers of fertile blood do not fit in my tiny womb.

"Suspecting this, the priests imagined with alarm that they would be forever burdened with a dwarf katami who reminded them at every moment of the mistake they had made in choosing me. As a result and after great arguments, they decided to take drastic action. One night the priestess who took care of my clothing in the chest came in and slit a dove's throat over me, staining my crotch and sheets with the blood. And then she left me there, in bed, without daring to move, sleepless and frightened with the blood drying on my thighs and tightening my skin.

"At daybreak they entered to get me up like they did every day and upon discovering the spots, they began the usual ritual of impurity, the katami's final liturgy. They gently stripped me of my fine clothing and of the luminous gold with which they had adorned me for all those years. They gave me a good cotton robe and a purse with copper coins— very little. And they left me at the door of the temple in the middle of the dusty street. They all acted as if they truly believed that the blood was mine and not the dove's. Perhaps there were priests and priestesses who overlooked the deception, or perhaps they preferred to believe the mendacious narration of the incident rather than the actual incident itself. The story told about an event often becomes more real than reality.

"I returned home, and my family took me in affectionately. But old katamis cause concern among the neighbors, and no man would ever dare to marry one of them because they feared being struck dead if they made love with an ex-goddess. As a result no one talked to me; no one smiled at me; no one came near me. Until I got tired of enduring the fearful silences and the evasive glances, and I left with some puppeteers who performed for the kings in the mountains and who announced me as the smallest woman in the world. From the puppeteers, I moved on to carnies, and from the carnies to a circus, now in the West. And in the circus I learned stage magic, which is not real magic, but rather illusionism: the acts with the cords that are cut but not cut, daggers that are driven in but not driven in, cards that appear and disappear. The tricks that I did with your grandfather and that you have seen me repeat with Segundo.

"When I was a katami, I always had to be at the disposal of the faithful. The believers came to the temple at all hours, and they made offerings of flower petals, wheat, and incense. The pilgrims, and those that had made a promise, paid with some coins, whatever they could afford, what they had and could donate, and they asked to see me. Then they were shown to the interior courtyard, which was narrow and dark with large pavers – damp stones consumed by mildew. They waited there patiently until I appeared at a little window on the second floor, behind the carved wooden lattice of the hallway. And I appeared: flowing red silks, shimmering of gold. I anchored myself to the window sill, and I gazed at them undaunted, aware of my divinity, granting them the grace of my look. And they, my faithful, adored me. In the dark well of that stone courtyard, they appealed to me with the intense love of necessity. They lifted their eyes toward me, and their hands, and their hearts, always asking for something; murmuring my name once and again. I know that by calling my name, they made me a goddess. We as humans all carry the possibility of being divine within us, and also the possibility of being devilish. In that dismal and gloomy courtyard, I succeeded at being a goddess. I don't know if one day I will tell you about them, but on other occasions, I became a devil."

CHAPTER FOURTEEN

Since that meeting with Portuguese, I stopped going out in the Neighborhood. I stopped going out, eating, sleeping, and I almost stopped breathing. I was terrified. When Grandmother or Amanda sent me on some errand, first I tried to pass it off on Chico, and if that failed, I had no other option than to carry out the order; I went the whole way in a hurry looking back over my shoulder to see if someone was following me. The scene in Portuguese's house had plunged me into some sort of paralysis. I had not told anyone about it, nor had I started to look for the money, like the man had commanded. I kept calm waiting for the sky to shatter right over my head while the only thing that remained alive in me was my own fear. That is how I spent the days, and we were getting closer and closer to the end of the world.

Until it arrived—in effect, the fateful day—because if there is something certain in this uncertain world, it is that time always slips away, and the end always seizes us. And so, one day they came to the door. It was an innocent time of day, eleven or perhaps twelve, the time when the gas meter readers come, or letter carriers, and Amanda opened the door without stopping to think. I saw her from the far end of the hallway; I saw how Amanda took a step back and straightened up; I knew from that very instant that things were going bad. One second later the visitors crossed the threshold, and I recognized them: it was Portuguese and the Shark. They stood planted in the middle of the entry way, with wide stances and small, with cold smiles on their awful faces. Amanda lifted her hands toward her face and left them dangling limply halfway, like she always did.

"Good morning," said Portuguese gently, sugarcoating his words. "Is Segundo here?"

Amanda shook her head.

"Fine," said the Shark, showing his yellow teeth, "Well, we'll stay and wait for him." He stretched out his arm, and completely naturally, he closed the entrance door behind him. Amanda seemed to recover her voice after that gesture.

"He... he is not going to come back," she muttered.

"Did you hear that, Portuguese?" the Shark said ironically, "She says Segundo is not coming back."

"What a shame," the other played along. "We were really longing to see him."

At that moment he turned around and discovered me.

"What a surprise! But, yes, my little friend is here."

He came toward me. I closed my eyes: Baba, don't let him reach me. Baba, make him evaporate into thin air in the middle of the hallway. Make a hole open up in the floor. Make the house disappear. Let us all die. I felt an iron hand on my forearm. I opened my eyes and two centimeters from my face was Portuguese licking his torn lip.

"I have been waiting for you. You failed me. That's not good," he said gently.

Amanda fluttered about uselessly over his shoulder like a distressed sparrow, trying to prevent the eggs from being stolen from her nest, "Get out of here... What did you come looking for... Leave us alone... Let go of the girl... I'm going to call the police," she sniveled with a trace of a voice.

They didn't pay any attention to her. I saw how the Shark tore the phone off the wall, and then, how he began to search everything systematically: the reception desk from the old boarding house, the built-in electrical box. I couldn't see Portuguese anymore because he lifted me in the air hanging by just one arm. I screamed.

"Where is it?" he growled, "Let's finish this at once; I'm tired."

Everything was very hazy. I think Amanda tried to rescue me, and I think that Portuguese knocked her down with one cuff in the face with his free hand because I saw Amanda sitting on the floor among loads of cats; the Shark must have opened the door to the cat room. And Airelai, who had been woken from her daytime slumber by the commotion, was also there. Everyone was shouting; I probably was, too, and now Amanda, Airelai, and I were together, and the Shark was asking us one more time for the damn money.

Suddenly there was a silence that was so complete that I could hear the furious pulsing of my heart against my ribs. At first I didn't understand why everyone had become so still; then I followed the gaze of the two men, and I saw my Grandmother's imposing figure. Grandmother Barbara was in the hall, next to the door to her room, dressed in a dark green outfit, bony and standing tall, letting her threatening look roll down the bridge of her powerful nose. It didn't seem strange to me that the men had become paralyzed; her presence froze my blood as well.

"Let's go," Portuguese smiled, and his purple and pink scar twisted up. "She's not going to scare us with this little game."

Then I discovered that Grandmother had a very small, silver pistol in her hand.

"That gun isn't real... And you wouldn't pull the trigger either, right, grandma?" said the Shark.

"Of course not..." said Portuguese.

But it was obvious that he thought that, yes, she could do it. He dried his palms on his pant leg; he cleared his throat, "Fine... Let's go."

The two walked slowly down the hallway, strutting with as much pride as if they were in a parade, waiting for the final applause of the spectators. They passed by Grandmother without looking at her and opened the door. Before leaving, Portuguese smoothed his thin hair; he patted his lapels looking for an invisible thread, and for no apparent reason, he delayed endlessly. Then he looked at the duchess Ines Garcia Meneses, a fat cat with a bald tail who had come out to the entryway to see why there was so much noise, and he said threateningly, enunciating each syllable, "We will come back."

And he left, following the Shark out the door. The dwarf woman ran to close the door and locked the deadbolt. Chico came out from under the couch, where he had been hiding. Grandmother lowered the pistol. Amanda burst into tears. I breathed. And for a long while, none of us did more than that, Airelai leaning against the recently closed door, Grandmother pointing toward the floor, Chico crouching near the couch, Amanda hiccupping, and me breathing. Motionless, the dwarf woman finally spoke, with a hoarse voice, "They will come back."

Amanda's moans became worse.

"The last time you didn't let him get away," Airelai added.

"The last time there was just one. And I was younger," Grandmother Barbara answered.

"And besides Maximo was there," the dwarf woman said in a whisper.

Grandmother nodded her head, "Yes ... Maximo was there."

She sighed and put the small pistol her pocket, "But if they want war, they will have war," she said raising her voice. "I am a dangerous enemy."

CHAPTER FIFTEEN

Since war had been declared, we went out a lot. Grandmother Barbara made a special effort so that the enemy would see us carry on a normal life, and so we did a bunch of unusual things that we had never done before, such as take walks all together or go out for ice cream at Rita's shop. This was what Grandmother called "a show of force."

"In the end all wars are won with psychological pressure," she would repeat.

But she always carried her exquisite little pistol, and she had the house secured with an alarm and reinforced locks.

Some days after the hostilities began, some politicians from the city arrived in the Neighborhood. They came to unveil a park, or rather to open it. It was in the east of the Neighborhood where the barren orchards and fields were overgrown with thistles. There was a huge house that I had seen while roaming around; it had stone walls that extended for hundreds of meters and closed in an exotic park that had been the whim of some nobility who had already passed away. The small palace was abandoned and nearly in ruins, but the park had been cared for very carefully, and the politicians were opening it for the public now. It was a little far for Grandmother Barbara, who did not like to walk too much, but given that we were in the middle of our psychological offense, she decided that we would go see it. Even the dwarf woman joined the expedition, even though she barely had time to sleep that day.

We arrived there in the middle of the afternoon when the ceremony had already ended and the sun was roasting the dusty fields. We arrived, and we went in, and it was like diving into a sea of vegetation. I believe that I had never been in such a beautiful place before. Enormous trees that whispered above our heads, small, green mossy hills, trembling ferns, a brook that babbled into a lake. We sat on the shore under a chestnut tree in the cool, perfumed shade.

"Look at the water," said Grandmother.

We looked at it. Before us, the pool's surface was burning with a golden fire. We were in the shadow, and the sun was throwing sparks of light at us from the water.

"It's like the sea," murmured Grandmother Barbara. She even seemed moved by the place.

There were so many people, but not so many that they were bothersome. To the right two teenagers were kissing. In the background a young woman was lying down with a baby who was almost naked sleeping on her stomach. To the left a black dog splashed around happily at the edge of the lake looking for a branch. He found it, took it and shook it out enthusiastically, and a million drops sparkled in the air around him. It didn't seem real. It didn't seem like the Neighborhood.

But, yes, it was because we suddenly saw Portuguese. At first we thought that he was following us, and we were startled. But we immediately noticed his surprise; he wasn't expecting to find us there either. He came from the other side of the trees and walked at a brisk pace toward the park's exit; with his brow furrowed, his bruised scar, and his gold tooth shining brightly. When he recognized us, he quickened his pace; the pale woman with her ear cut off was behind him, half running. She was more pale than ever, almost ashen, with the boy clutched to her chest. The two crossed near us and left the park through the back exit, and they disappeared in the charred, desert terrain. Where would they be going that way, that would take them to that abandoned, dry plain.

lay down on my back. The grass pinched my neck, my ears, my bare arms and legs. The green leaves and little pieces of sky made a lace above my head. The silence was full of murmurs, and the air was full of scents: the perfume of the wood, the shadows, and the heat. The sunny tree-lined avenues of childhood.

"Let's go see the other side of the lake," said Amanda.

"No, no...wait a little longer," answered Grandmother Barbara.

Grandmother could never leave the places she liked. While the rest of us were walking, exploring, and discovering, she was still eager and engrossed as she remained glued to the first rock. Airelai would say that this was because she could not bear the loss of lovely moments, and that each time she left a landscape that touched her, she felt a little closer to her death. Now she was here anchored to the first chestnut tree of the first slope of the first shore that we had found upon entering the park; she spent hours there, and she didn't move. Chico, Amanda, the dwarf woman, and I went to see the rest of the grounds. We laughed a lot, we caught a cricket, and Chico fell into the water; and when we returned to the first shore, Grandmother was still there like a sphinx in the same position.

I sat next to her. It was growing dark; the earth smelled like warm flesh, and the grass trembled under my fingers. I looked at Grandmother Barbara; a transparent, round tear, which reflected the roundness of the world upside down, ran down her cheek.

"Why are you crying?" I asked.

"Because I will remember all this in my last moment."

And I didn't understand her because, even though I had already discovered what death was, on that most lovely afternoon, I had forgotten.

CHAPTER SIXTEEN

After the visit by Portuguese and the Shark, the dwarf woman, who had figured out that I was keeping quiet about something, caught me when we were alone and made me tell her everything I knew. I spoke to her about my forays in the Neighborhood and my incident in Casas Chicas and about Portuguese's demands and threats. Airelai listened to it all with utmost attention, and from time to time she asked specific questions to clarify details. When I stopped talking, she remained thoughtful for a long while.

"Would you be able to identify Portuguese's shack?" she asked finally.

"Of course," I was surprised.

"And would you be capable of leading me there?"

"No! No! He'll kill us."

"Don't worry; I'm not going to endanger you or me. I just want to take a quick look to check a few things. We'll go at night when no one will see us, and on top of that we'll be under a spell – a very powerful, ancient talisman, which will take care of us and condemn that bastard. So don't be afraid because we will be protected by magic."

The dwarf woman said that, but it didn't leave me very convinced because my fear of Portuguese was greater than my faith. But while she was carefully preparing our foray (no one was supposed to find out), Airelai began to explain the various levels of existing spells to me. So she told me about the primary spells, which never fail and whose effectiveness has been proven irrefutably for many centuries, but which no magician should ever abuse because they are so powerful that they suck a bit of life from the user. Then there are the secondary spells, and tertiary, and fourth, and even simple enchantments without any level, that are commonly known as magician's kisses, which are witchcraft of little value and that often fail but have the advantage of leaving no trace in the sorcerer's consciousness or memory.

"To illustrate my point, a wizard who only had done these simple enchantments his whole life would be innocent like a child," the dwarf woman explained to me, "But of course, there are no wizards like that."

I listened, completely absorbed, and she persuaded me more and more about her power. And when she told me that she was going to use a primary spell for our fearful trip to Casas Chicas, all the fear and doubts I had faded; I became convinced that the objective of our journeey was to put a hex on that damn Portuguese and making mincemeat of him, ending this war once and for all.

A couple of days later Airelai decided that that same night we would go to the outskirts of the Neighborhood on the south side. After dinner, the dwarf woman prepared a delicious infusion of herbs that everyone except me and her drank appreciatively. Soon

Chico, Amanda, and Grandmother Barbara were walking around the house, yawning and wanting to go to bed because the infusion had valerian root and other secret herbs and roots that result in a sweet, calm slumber. So I pretended to lay down like everyone else, and the dwarf woman began to get ready like she did every night before going wherever she went at night. But soon everyone was breathing heavily, and I had no problem getting up.

I found Airelai in her room, sitting on her trunk, writing a spell on a piece of paper. The paper was very good and heavy, but yellowing a bit, and it was delicately cut into the shape of a five pointed star. In the heart of the star, the dwarf woman wrote the following words:

S	A	T	O	R
A	R	E	P	O
T	E	N	E	T
O	P	E	R	A
R	O	T	A	S

Then she folded the paper and put it in the pocket of the tiny, tight black pants she was wearing.

"That's it. Nothing can happen to us now."

"Why can you read it in all directions? And why can't you understand more than two words?" I asked, excited.

"In reality, you don't even understand those two words, silly; they're not what you think because the spell is in Latin, which is one of the noble languages for magic. The other two are Arabic and Hebrew. But you don't need to know too much; it's dangerous. It's enough that you know that it is a very good spell – first class. We're completely safe."

Convinced of that, we went out to the street, and I lead Airelai through the gloomy Neighborhood without hesitation. The dwarf woman was dressed in all black, and I, who didn't have clothes that color, wore jeans and a navy blue t-shirt. I felt protected by the spell and by the night's shadows; we were walking through the dark streets without making noise like two shreds of mist and fog. The few people that we met didn't even seem to see us. The magic was working.

Soon we arrived at the top of Violet Street, which now that it was night, was indeed reddish violet, and it was shining with a frozen, ghostly light. I stopped at the corner without going onto the street; the sidewalks were full of men.

"What are you doing? Come; keep moving forward," grumbled the dwarf woman.

"If we take Violet Street, it will be much shorter," I said.

"You can't go on this street at night. Haven't you learned that yet?"

"Why can't you? Is it because of that light?"

"You want to know so much," the dwarf woman joked. "You want to know everything, and that is impossible. In order to survive, it's always necessary to keep some secret. Keep one part hidden—the part that is precisely who you truly are. Because our exterior appearance corresponds to what others know of us, but in reality we are what others do not know of us. And so above all, I am what you don't know of me; in the same way that Jack the Ripper was above all Jack the Ripper even though in the world he was, according to what they say, a relative of the Queen of England."

I was affected and kept reflecting on Airelai's words because I feared that all people were hiding a murderer inside. I was so caught up thinking about all that, I didn't notice the minutes escaping from me, and when I realized it, we found ourselves at the far edge of the Neighborhood, next to the gravelly area and garbage dumps. There were no more street lights here, so the dwarf woman took out a small flashlight. At night the hills of debris and waste seemed larger, and the rotten smell was more intense. Everything the flashlight illuminated was repulsive and dirty: broken tires, greasy cans, foul-smelling, unspeakable substances. The world had become a nightmare of garbage and debris, and we were lost walking inside that bad dream. But the spell gave us the strength to keep walking.

We finally reached the steep slope; we turned off the flashlight and we stopped to look at Casas Chicas at our feet. The camp of shacks seemed to sleep but there were a few lights; none were very bright. Paying close attention, one could see some shadows wandering about. As our eyes were getting accustomed to the darkness, we could see that nearly all the people were making either their way toward or coming from the same area of the shantytown. Many went alone, and others two by two, but it didn't seem like they were talking to each other. They came out of the heaps of garbage like specters, passing before us without looking at us. They staggered down the embankment, and they made their way to that specific area in the shantytown that seemed to stir so much interest. A little later, they could be seen leaving – almost running. Some went up the embankment again and disappeared in the night, but others let themselves fall to the ground as soon as they crossed past the last row of shacks. Next to a broken washbasin with a faucet, they handled something with their head down for a long time. A woman stuck her head out of the window of the closest dwelling, she yelled an insult, threatened the head-down shadows by the basin with her fist. She threw two blunt objects at them, one after the other; I don't know if they were rocks or cans. But the figures stayed curled up, keeping to themselves. The woman's curses boomed in the hot night and then she slammed the little window. Darkness and silence fell over us once again.

"Now I can see," said the dwarf woman. "Which one is Portuguese's house?"

"It's over that way. We would have to go down there."

"Well let's go."

"What?"

"Well, we'll act naturally. As you'll see, there are a lot of people," answered Airelai.

And she stood up and started to descend the embankment. I hurried to follow her because I was frightened of being left alone and far from the spell that Airelai had in her pocket. We crossed a few meters from the washbasin, and no one looked at us. We entered the shantytown, and an old man with white hair and a wooden cane spit at our feet with contempt.

"And now dwarfs, too," he grunted.

Airelai didn't bat an eyelash, so neither did I. I was trying to remember the exact location of Portuguese's house. It wasn't easy because all the shacks looked the same. I began to suspect that I was not going to be able to identify the spot.

"Let's follow that one," murmured Airelai.

She was referring to a guy who had gone down the embankment before us. We dropped behind him, and we moved forward through the dark camp. There were no lights, but there were eyes, and those eyes were looking at us, shining in the obscurity from the open doors of the shacks; it was too hot to close up the houses. The whole time I was waiting for someone to shout at us for being intruders, for someone to stop us, for someone to throw us out of there, for those eyes to come out and glare at us with daggers. But no one moved in the sticky, foul-smelling night.

The man who we followed was thin and had a green, long-sleeve shirt; he stopped in front of the only door that was closed.

He knocked three times and whispered something. They opened the door, and a sliver of light fell on the dirty gravel of the camp. The man went in, and the door shut at his back.

"That's Portuguese's house!" I said almost yelling, excited by the discovery.

"Are you sure?"

"Yes, yes! I think that his wife was the one who opened the door."

The door cracked open again, and the guy with the green shirt came out, and this time we could see Portuguese in the middle of the threshold under the light.

"We're going to stay here a little while," said the dwarf woman.

We were hidden behind the rusty skeleton of a broken refrigerator: a good spot given that we were small. From there we had a view of the entrance to the shack and we could see the trickle of visitors that Portuguese had. They were almost all men, and in general they seemed young, although a couple of them had a wasted, sickly appearance. We were gazing at the hustle and bustle for a long time, and the visitors never stayed in the shack more than four or five minutes.

"We've seen everything," said the dwarf woman. "We can leave."

It seemed odd to me that Airelai didn't do any magical sleight of hand, that she didn't take the talisman out of her pocket, nor did she conjure up lightning and storms over Portuguese's head, but I supposed that the spell was already over and that the dwarf woman had put a curse on his body. So we got up and backtracked through the narrow, wretched alleyways full of eyes; we went up the embankment, and we stopped out of breath at the top of the steep slope.

"Nothing happened to us," I marveled.

And the dwarf woman answered, "Of course not."

But I think I noticed relief in her elated tone. Before returning home, we circled the rim of the steep slope, considering the perspective of Casas Chicas from up high, like generals who delight in observing the camp of a defeated enemy. We went along without light; the bright glow of the full moon began to filter through the clouds and made reflections pool on the tin roofs. I was looking at those roofs when I tripped on something and fell flat on my face on the ground. Or rather on a dark, soft bundle. At first glance I was able to discern a pale ear in the shadows: a human being. I shrieked while I was still on all fours, and Airelai ran to cover my mouth.

"Quiet! What happened?"

I didn't have to answer because the body's presence was imposing. Airelai pushed it with the tip of her foot; it was stiff. At that moment the full moon appeared completely. The hills of garbage were sparkling as if someone had inlaid jewels in the muck. Under that livid, metallic light, the cadaver seemed more helpless; it was a small body hunched over itself. Airelai leaned over it and turned it around. It revolved with bent knees as if it were made of wood. I immediately recognized his slanted, fleshy eyes that lacked eyelashes and now lacked expression. He seemed more childlike dead; seeing him that way – so defenseless and small – I was astonished that I had been afraid of him. He still had a syringe stuck in his arm, and his t-shirt was hard from the dried blood. The dwarf woman got down on her knees next to him and closed his eyes, but one of his thick, obstinate eyelids opened again. Airelai put out her hand to close it again, but she seemed to change her mind halfway, and she got up.

"Let's go," she said with a shudder.

A colossal roar resounded at that moment, and over the airport's gate, right on top of Casas Chicas, the nose of an airplane appeared; it was an enormous, dazzling ship that was growing and growing above us, and moved forward through the air, millimeter by millimeter, with miraculous lethargy. That iron bird bellowed over our heads, taking up the entire sky, like a dragon in the night, like a silver whale under the full moon, letting its powerful metallic belly slip over us. It was so close that it seemed that we could brush against it just by stretching out our arms. But we never would have dared touch that god of the sky and of the darkness – that beautiful panting monster who rose crackling into the sea of the heavens above the dwarf woman, above me, and above the dead boy's only open eye.

CHAPTER SEVENTEEN

Perhaps Grandmother Barbara had the intuition that that night was going to be crucial, or perhaps she already had found out about Segundo. Be that as it may, before we left the house, she called me to her room and had me button up the top of her gray silk dress. A favor that I knew she didn't need because I had seen her put on that dress without anyone's help other times. I got up on a chair; I fastened the hooks and smoothed out the lace a little.

"That's it."

Grandmother turned around and grabbed my chin with her cold, hard hand.

"You've grown," she declared, "and your face has changed."

She looked at me with such a fixed stare as if she had to copy my features by heart onto paper, but at the same time, she seemed not to see me. She let go of me and she started searching for something in her dresser drawer.

"Are you happy with us?" she said.

It was a very difficult question, and I began to reflect on it earnestly, but when I finally came to a conclusion, I realized that my Grandmother wasn't waiting for an answer. She had continued taking out handkerchiefs and moving little boxes in her dresser. Finally her hand closed over something.

"I want to give you a gift. A very special gift. A true gift. One to be remembered."

She opened her fist, and a drop of water was shining brightly in her palm. It was a small crystal ball, clear and transparent like air, but in its center there was cloudy, iridescent speck—a milky whirlwind. The crystal was hanging on a long silver chain that was blackened by disuse.

"It's gorgeous." I was amazed.

"Put it on. And wear it always. And remember me when you look at it."

The chain was so long that I had to wrap it around my neck twice. The ball was heavy even though it was so small, and it remained cold even though the temperature was suffocating. It seemed very elegant to me, the perfect accessory for an evening party. Because that night was the Neighborhood party, and there was a festival in the square across from Rita's shop. And Grandmother, who was still immersed in her war strategy of being seen, had decided that we should go. To her, the event was nothing more than another skirmish, but for me, it was my first public, evening party. I was excited.

We went out after dinner—Amanda, Chico, Grandmother Barbara, and I were all dressed to the nines. The main Neighborhood street was decorated with streamers and banners, and it didn't seem as ugly as it was during the day. The square's terrace was also all decked out, and they had put up festive lights.

On the corner there was a small carousel, to which Chico dragged Amanda immediately; there were also a couple of stands for target shooting, a lotto, and churro stand. Deafening music was coming from loud speakers that were hanging high on a post.

"I'm going to sit there. You all go do whatever you want," Grandmother Barbara said.

Next to the wall there were two or three benches and some folding chairs, and there were still some free. I went toward the carousel looking for Chico and Amanda, and on the way, I met Airelai. She appeared between the people's legs like a specter, and she grabbed my arm nervously, and put her lips close to my ear.

"Now you don't have to be afraid of Portuguese," she whispered. "And much less of the Shark."

Having said that, she disappeared again in the crowd, leaving me intrigued and confused. There were a lot of people, people who I had seen before, and some who were completely new. The youngsters were yelling and chasing each other; the adults were talking or dancing. I yelled and ran around with Chico and the other kids, too, and we sang and shouted until we were hoarse. There was a kind of broad truce in effect, and all the gangs from different areas were tolerating each other without any attacks though they stuck together on different corners of the square, and they were careful not to ask girls from a rival gang to dance. Even on the night of the party, the old codes were in play, and in order to enjoy the festival without mishaps, one had to know the unspoken rules. But we—Chico and I—knew them well, so we played and laughed, and we were happy.

Early in the morning, I was quite exhausted and sat on the curb to rest. The night was sticking to my skin like a soft, warm veil; a light breeze occasionally carried the smell of frying oil from the nearby churro stand. My feet hurt, and my head was in the clouds: from the party, from weariness, and from the excitement. A cloud of dust floated between the dancers' legs, but that bit of freshness that dawn brings and which announces the arrival of a new day, was struggling to infuse in the warm air. It was one of those complete, carnal summer nights when time stands still.

"Do you want a soda? I'll give you one."

I looked over my shoulder, and I saw Rita, the one from the shop. Rita had taken a couple of folding tables, a few buckets of ice, and a whole slew of beer and sodas out from her shop, and she had spent the entire night working. Now that the clientele was thinning, she could allow herself some time to chitchat. She must have done good business because you could see she was in a good mood.

"Thank you," I said standing up and accepting the drink.

A few meters away on the benches, Amanda, Chico, and Grandmother were drinking hot chocolate with churros. Grandmother Barbara gestured to let me know that we were leaving soon. I nodded.

"I don't like it," Rita was saying to me in the meantime. "I know that he has been to your house many times, but he is not trustworthy. I don't like him."

I looked at her completely lost without knowing what she was talking about, and I followed her eyes, and I saw Portuguese on the other side of the square.

"Portuguese!" I exclaimed without being able to hold back.

But, how was it possible? Hadn't the dwarf woman said that I shouldn't be afraid of him? And nevertheless, the man seemed perfectly fine. He was leaning on the wall with a plastic glass in his hand, and his domineering, disdainful attitude was more domineering and disdainful than all the cocky guys from all the gangs from all the Neighborhood areas that were here.

"That one," Rita continued. "That measly character. It seems untrue that he had dealings with your family, with your grandmother there, who is a real lady. But of course, one has children, and she has children. You can't control your kid's lives. If one goes awry on you, it's like the opposite of winning the lottery. You can't fix it. If you gamble, you can't help being affected; and with children, you're always gambling. You have all the raffle tickets for tragedy."

Besides having made a big profit, Rita must have had a few drinks because she was more talkative than usual.

"In a shop you see a lot of the world. There is a lot of culture at the counter. Before this I worked at an American bar, so I know it well. People arrive, and they tell you things. You see everything; you hear everything; you know everything. The world passes by while you stand still. That's why you can think, and connect one tiny detail with another. For example, do you know why Portuguese's mouth was slashed? Well because he talked. Because he is more of a stool pigeon more than anyone. They say he told what he shouldn't have, and they smashed his teeth out with a hammer and cut his lip into slices, and that's why he fled his city and came here. Your necklace is very pretty. It looks like a crocodile tear."

At that moment there was a special silence on the terrace. That is to say, there was still noise: the din of the music, the splutter of food frying, some child's cry, but all who were present were holding their breath, and the night seemed to have crystallized. And all this interest, this commotion, and this tension was provoked by Segundo. By Segundo, who had appeared suddenly in the square, and who was now standing in the middle of the terrace, gazing at the scene slowly and coldly while the people moved surreptitiously away from him and left him in a circle of loneliness and fear.

Segundo came fueled with determination, with icy fury, and with triumph. The violence that emanated from him reached all the corners of the square in slow waves, poisoning the air. He was planted firmly in his wide stance; he was a large, thick man, and a massive, still fresh cut was shining on his right cheek—a swollen, red cut that seemed to open a monstrous mouth over his cheek.

It all happened then as if it had been foreseen and rehearsed without no more surprises for anyone, other than Segundo's astonishing arrival. Segundo had not moved from the center of the square and began to search the whole perimeter of the terrace with his gaze, and when his eyes fell on Portuguese, the latter turned pale; he sucked on his broken lip nervously and took off running like a ferret darting through the crowd, zigzagging to hide himself between the people, with his belly almost touching the ground. Those near him gasped in astonishment. Curtain—end of act one.

Segundo's cold eyes continued to roll over the people and things, and finally they stopped with a brief flicker on the benches by the wall: on Grandmother Barbara, who, sitting tall, mirroring him with the same defiant look, and at Amanda, who was shaking excessively. He must not have seen Chico because I could barely distinguish him at first; the boy had already camouflaged himself, like a chameleon, with the color of the wall.

Then Segundo went in motion, and those present held their breath again. In a few calm strides, the man covered the distance that separated him from the benches; he leaned over Amanda, took her by the hand and pulled her up gently. Amanda let him lift her like a feather; she gazed at her husband with her eyes so round she seemed like a doll—she wasn't even blinking. Then Segundo put his arms around her and squeezed her against him, and lifting her up—she was light and almost fainting—began to dance with her to the music that was coming from the loud speakers.

Segundo turned and turned with the woman in his arms, lit by the paper lanterns' blinking lights. He offered alternately the view of his horrible disfigured cheek and that of his intact profile, a profile that was like he always did, yet in some way new, stronger, darker, like one who keeps a horrific secret, but also more attractive, with a fiery, hellish attraction. And Segundo was repulsive and handsome at the same time and danced while Amanda looked at him, not as someone who recognizes but rather as someone who remembers, perhaps lost in the intoxication of the spins, in the delight of those strong arms, the memory of other dances and other velvet nights like this one.

Those present let out their breaths, relieved or perhaps disappointed after realizing that nothing happened. And seeing Segundo's progress on the terrace, little by little, those nearby began to pair up to dance, like what happens in the ballrooms of castles in stories, when the prince and princess open the waltz and then all the guests join in, with steps and spins that become more and more dizzy and giddy. In the same way the whole Neighborhood joined Segundo and Amanda's dance, and soon the whole terrace was full of dancing couples. But they were the couple of honor that night and also, among all the others, the ones who danced with the most fierceness and the most refinement.

CHAPTER EIGHTEEN

That night, after the festival, we all went home together, crushed by a toxic silence that was overflowing with unspoken questions. Once there Chico and I ran straight to bed, seeking the shelter of the sheets. I tried to stay awake to listen in case something happened, but I was so tired I fell asleep. Shortly thereafter I woke up to screaming; Amanda was shaking me, her face contorted, with the boy in her arms.

"Run! Run!" she was shouting at me, while Chico was whimpering half asleep. "Follow me and don't stop to grab anything!"

I followed her, dazed by my slumber, not knowing what was happening. We went into the hallway, and then I smelled the smoke and saw the flames lick the door of the room with the couch. My head cleared at once. We went out in a mad rush, and into the vestibule where Grandmother was running with the dwarf woman's help. We threw ourselves down the stairs between the infernal heat and a shower of tiny embers. The wooden stairs were smoking. Fortunately, there was no more than one floor, and we soon got outside. On the sidewalk a good number of people had congregated. Segundo was in front of everyone. Amanda was only wearing a slip; Grandmother, a robe; the dwarf woman, a t-shirt; and me, my underwear and my crystal sphere with the silver chain. But Segundo was completely dressed. Before us the small house was steaming and cracking loudly, as if the burning were painful. Then we heard an explosion, and the breath of fire appeared suddenly in a window. It was like the signal at the beginning of a race; flames on different corners immediately emerged, and the entire building was a torch in minutes.

Grandmother burst into tears, and that rare show of weakness in her made me grasp the gravity of the catastrophe.

"My clothes, my things..." moaned Grandmother Barbara.

"We'll buy more. We'll buy everything – it will be new and better," roared Segundo ferociously without taking his eyes of the fire.

"My photos..."

"We don't need those old photos at all."

The enormous blaze crackled before us, tightening the skin on our cheeks with its scorching breath and spewing a stream of sparks into the night. None of us who were present could avert our eyes from the violent, bright fire; the one who was the most absorbed in the show was Segundo himself, who seemed to want to drink in that hellish scene.

The beams splintered, and the blackened window frames were shrieking, but it was useless because the flames were devouring the house with quick bites. The firefighters arrived after a while when the building had already collapsed, and nothing was left to save. With them came a gray-haired man, who approached Segundo and began to gaze at the fire next to him.

"What bad luck you have," he said apathetically after a while. "This is the second fire now."

Segundo kept watching the flames, showing no sign of having heard him. The man pulled his pants up at the waist. He had a small belly, a very dirty shirt, and a wrinkled jacket.

"You've already been tried as an arsonist," the guy continued.

"And I was acquitted," answered Segundo calmly, without turning his head.

The two were quiet for a while, and then I believe I saw the gray-haired man's eyes meet those of the dwarf woman.

"This really doesn't matter to me. You know?" he finally said with the same apathy. "I'm tied up with other matters. With a certain Portuguese, and with his business. Some very dirty business, of course. Now that I think of it, someone told me that you know him. Portuguese. That there was a time when you were friends."

He took a wrinkled cigarette from his shirt pocket; he lit it and took a few slow, calm puffs. For a few minutes, only the roar of the fire could be heard.

"You know, I'm going to tell you a strange story that I heard," the man carried on casually. "A few weeks ago, a guy from outside came to stick his nose in Neighborhood business. A huge man with bad teeth. Well then he disappeared; he vanished. I heard there was a fight, that knives were drawn, and that someone killed him. It's not that it matters to me; I won't cry for him, I assure you. But, you see, I have this obsession with finding things out. Of course, you wouldn't know anything about him, right?"

Segundo didn't answer.

"No, of course not," the man answered himself. And then after a short pause, "And how did you rip your face like that? It's a very ugly slash... You see, I like your brother's scar better. It's more elegant.

More manly."

Having said that, he threw the cigarette on the ground and left. Segundo clenched his jaw; I saw his muscles twitch next to his ears. He was next to me: tall and strapping, a few feet taller than me. The pyre lit up his eyes and reflected in his face, making the injury on his cheek look green; it looked like it was bleeding in the glow. His was an intense, sinister face capped off by a wreath of smoke. A somber face that reminded me of something, perhaps a time in the past, perhaps a nightmare, a bad dream about smoke and shrieks, a fire breathing dragon in my face. I shuddered. At my side, Segundo took a step forward and spit on the bonfire. Next he turned, crowned by the fire like a demon. Then, I could see his whole face well. He was laughing.

CHAPTER NINETEEN

The dwarf woman, who knew a lot about sizes and relative volumes, was fascinated by the Earth's largest living being, the whale. Airelai would always say that she was captivated by those colossal, sweet creatures who were so light in the sea yet sad prisoners of gravity on the shores where they were sometimes beached, for some puzzling reason and ended up dying due to their own size. And one afternoon that summer the dwarf woman told us the following story:

"You should know that whales possess a huge brain; proportionately, it is ten times bigger than a human brain. Therefore, they are very intelligent animals, and despite being powerful, they are not aggressive. That's what I admire most about whales, and even though they know and they are strong, they are peaceful. These tremendous creatures sing and communicate, and it seems that they have a very complex language. I know that they scream and cry. I know because I have heard them, and I have seen them, or rather, I have seen and heard one whale. It was a long time ago, but I cannot forget it. Once in a while I have to talk about it so that its memory will not burn in my mind."

"It happened in the West, during a dark, violent period of my life, which as I look back on it, seems to be the usual tone of existence with few exceptions. But back then I was so young that I still believed in periods of good and bad luck. For reasons that don't matter here, I happened to be in a little coastal city that wasn't noteworthy—its name was not even memorable. It was summer but the weather was extraordinarily cool with temperatures lower than they had been in decades. This must have influenced the cetacean's journey, or perhaps not, and it was simply a case of an adventurous individual. The fact is that the small fishing fleet came back to port towing a huge animal behind it; it was, amazingly, a whale, even though whales had never been seen on these coasts. The fishermen were moved by this unexpected finding, and they agreed to join forces and unite their little boats. With the help of their boat hooks, the harpoons used for catching octopus, and the peaceful innocence of the cetacean, they were able to spear the creature and tangle her up in cables and nets leaving her defenseless. And they towed her into the port like that: injured and captive.

"The whale's arrival meant a commotion in the city because the local people had never had the opportunity to see one up close. So they brought the animal to the old wood pier; they tied it to the piles with harpoon cables and they left it exposed so that everyone could see it. And they came—from the city and from the neighboring towns and from farms: whole families, gangs of teenagers, busses full of elderly people, housewives and fathers with their young children, kids who shrieked with delight and clapped their little hands while gazing at that fantastic being. In the meantime the whale struggled, trying to free itself, and thus drove the iron spears deeper into its body. Or else, exhausted, it would rock tamely in the cloudy water, with blood flowing from its many wounds. It had red blood, like we do.

"I have witnessed horrors that cannot be spoken. I have seen lame people stoned for being lame, blacks burned alive for being black, the elderly starved to death by their children, girls raped by their own fathers. I have seen throats slit for a pack of cigarettes and guts ripped out in the name of God. There are people who enjoy such hell, and I know them well because as a little person, I was forced to coexist with them. With the sadists. I suspect that we dwarf women attract cruel guys, like bright lights do to moths. Perhaps because we remind them of children, who are their favorite victims, or because they believe we're fragile. But I possess the gift, and I am powerful. That's why I have always survived them.

"Of all the types of cruelty I have known, the most widespread is that which disregards its own cruelty. That's how humans are – they destroy and torment, but they arrange things to believe they are innocent. And that is what happened with the cetacean. I happened to be at the port when the fleet returned, so I was one of the first people to see the whale. It's magnitude startled me; it was the length of the whole pier – from end to end. Its skin was brown and rough, with mollusks and anemones stuck to its sides, and if it remained still. It seemed like a rock more than an animal. But some place on that mass of flesh, there was a small eye that looked at the enemy world with anguish. Over time I learned to recognize the creature's different expressions and tones of voice. Because it shrieked. From that first morning the whale shrieked audibly as it was moored by the spears.

"Days passed, and the cetacean became so popular that the number of visitors grew, and a little industry was being organized. The Fisherman's Association began to charge an entrance fee at the pier the second week, and some sharp businesspeople set up a few booths with postcards, souvenirs, drinks, and snacks. There was even a photographer who took your portrait for a reasonable price in front of the prisoner's huge mass covered with spears.

"At first I went every afternoon to see her, and the Association's employees didn't charge me the entrance fee; they must have thought my behavior was odd, and possibly they thought that being a dwarf woman, I suffered from a certain degree of idiocy, like many crude souls tend to think of those who are different. I stayed for a long while with the whale, but the crowds, the laughter, and visitors' parties ended up cracking my nerves. Then I began to go at night when no one was there; I sat on the edge of the pier with my legs dangling, and I kept the animal company until dawn.

"Once in a while, more and more frequently, the whale struggled furiously against its ties; the harpoons became buried a little more deeply in its flesh; its wounds opened, and the water around her became red. I would talk to her softly, then and I advised her not to do that—that would only bring more pain. But she continued with her useless efforts; I think she didn't understand my language, or perhaps the hope of freedom was more important to her than the suffering. Even though she didn't understand my words and she didn't follow my advice, I was sure that my presence was some help to her. They were some lonely nights, and we spent them looking at each other. Her shrieks were heart-rending at times, and at others she trilled sweetly like a bird; perhaps she was talking to me about the other whales from the pod, about the pleasure of diving into the deep waters, or about the rich swaths of plankton in the beautiful sea in the North.

"One month of torture and then another went by. And my whale didn't die. I would have let her go, but it was impossible for me to untie or cut the steel cables. I would have killed her, but how could I kill such a large creature being so tiny myself. Her stony, beautiful skin was becoming cracked; it was no longer brown, but rather an ashen gray color. In the end, she barely moved; she had been tied to the pier for eighty-seven days, and the visitors were becoming scarce. Then the fishermen arrived in some motorboats, and they towed the creature toward the shore, until she was beached on the shore. And they began to chop her into pieces with their large knives.

"Since then I have read a lot about whales, looking in books to find some consolation after that horror. That's how I learned, for example, that a beached whale out of water passes away shortly because the weight of its own body collapses its lungs. But they began to chop her up immediately. She was still alive, and one has to cut a lot to reach the vital organs of a cetacean. Nevertheless, she didn't shriek. I think she did it for me so that I wouldn't hear her."

CHAPTER TWENTY

After the night of the Great Fire several things happened that changed our lives. In the first place, we had to move, given that the old boarding house had been reduced to charred ruins. We went to live across the street above the old club where Segundo and the dwarf woman did their magic show. It was a place that was much worse than where we lived before—a tiny apartment that was damp and dark and whose windows all opened onto a small interior courtyard that seemed like a well. Now there was no room for the cats, and Grandmother didn't have two rooms but rather just one—and a very small one at that—with a small bed pushed up against the wall, nothing like the majestic wooden bed from which Grandmother Barbara reigned over the old house. Segundo had reserved the best room for him and Amanda, but it wasn't anything special either. As for Chico and me, we shared a rickety old bed in a room so narrow it seemed to be a hallway. Segundo had lied when he had said that we would have better houses, better furniture, and a better life.

The dwarf woman slept downstairs in the dressing room at the club, in the same trunk as always. Curiously, someone had taken it, and all the other chests with props for magic out of the old boarding house before the fire. Those were the only things saved from the disaster. One day I heard Grandmother say to Airelai, "You knew about it."

Airelai's eyes were red, and her voice sounded odd and superficial. "They only told me that, from that day forward, I was going to live in the club," the dwarf woman answered, "And I, as you know well, obey."

Grandmother was unrecognizable. That was the second of the major changes that had happened in our lives; Grandmother Barbara no longer seemed like Grandmother Barbara. She no longer had her magnificent clothes, her smoking incense sticks, her lace pillows, her furniture, or the framed photos on the little table. She was much shorter now, but above all, she lacked something internal—that fiery, iron look that had shown in her eyes before. She spent hours missing her cats, and we never went to the cemetery anymore. Grandmother didn't go out at all now, and she got out of bed less each day. She was sick, or so she would say, though I couldn't force myself to believe it even when I could see she was so feeble and down. Grandmother Barbara, I still thought then, was great and indestructible, and this cloud of weakness couldn't be more than a fleeting illusion.

In the meanwhile, Segundo had also changed. He, on the other hand, seemed bigger and darker. His thick wrists protruded from his suits, which now looked small on him, and his skin was almost as black as his gaze. The scar on his cheek was healing—a bulging, shiny, pink groove now. When Segundo was very nervous, he scratched the cut with his thumb nail, and we soon learned this was the sign of a prelude to a domestic storm. One of the times that he was scratching his scar with determination, shortly after the Great Fire, Chico tiptoed out of the house and didn't come back. I mean night came, and he didn't return. He didn't show up the next day either, and even though the dwarf woman and Airelai covered the whole Neighborhood, they couldn't find him. Then Amanda went to the police, and a few hours later they arrived at our house with Chico and a woman who asked a lot of questions and who made Segundo sign some papers, which put him into the worst mood and made him scratch his scar more than ever. That was not a good day.

Since Segundo came back, we hadn't seen Portuguese or the Shark again. They said Portuguese was in some neighborhood in a nearby city. Or that's what Rita said, who assured us that she had found out from some relatives that she had in that area. "Seems that he's trying to make a life for himself in that neighborhood, but it's not going so well for him."

On the other hand, there was no news about the Shark; the earth had devoured him.

"That's how it is, kid. That is exactly what happened to that guy; the earth devoured him…" Rita would say, and she laughed and winked, as if it were a joke.

I went along with Rita because she was kind, and she would give us peppermints. But deep down I knew that both Portuguese and the Shark had been defeated by the dwarf woman's spell, and they were in some dark place imprisoned by the hex: inside a mountain for example, which is where, according to the stories that are told, the great witches tend to lock up their enemies. I never told anyone because I knew that you're not supposed to mention magic, but I felt proud to be the only one in the Neighborhood to know the truth.

You entered our apartment through the club, up a little staircase that was behind the curtain next to the stage. During the day, with the club closed, this was no problem. But at night, the noise, smoke and reddish glow came bouncing up the stairs. At first that underground world frightened me, then I learned to be more daring. Some nights I tiptoed down the stairs, and I could make out the magic show from behind the curtains—Airelai and Segundo were working in the club again. Through a crack I watched them bathed in that red air that seemed unbreathable, as they waved sparkling ribbons in the air and created a shower of stars out of nothing.

One dawn I had to go look for a medicine for Grandmother Barbara. Amanda had just awakened me from a deep sleep and, even though I was still dazed, I went down the stairs, opened the curtain, and without thinking, I dove into the warm, evil milieu. There were a lot of people and a lot of noise. I suppose the loudspeakers must have been blaring into my ears because what I remember is that the boom of the music came up through my legs and seized my belly as if it were seizing me, as if an invisible, giant trembling hand were climbing up my body. On the stage there were three naked women with their nipples flashing, and the air was a nightmare the color of blood. I ran toward the door. I had to push through men's backs and legs; they lowered their horrific faces toward me with wild looks, and their mouths muttering and reeking of alcohol.

Since then I had to make the same journey several times; I was always afraid and distressed, but I overcame it. Living above the club, I discovered the enormous difference between the venue during the day and at night, between the dirty warehouse that the empty club was and the hopeless, sweaty swarm that it became very late at night. And I learned something essential—that hell is not a place, but rather a state. A poison we all carry within.

CHAPTER TWENTY-ONE

"It's the birds, the black birds," mumbled Grandmother from her bed. "Listen to how they flap their wings, those wretched birds. They're the black birds who are coming to find me."

They weren't birds, but rather airplanes. The airplanes passed above us and made all the windows of the dismal courtyard rattle. There were large, heavy airplanes that flew very low; one could see their fatigue in their sluggish movements and the noise they made, which was like the parsimonious grating of a huge rock dragging along. There were others that were like tiny, nervous mosquitoes— just a distant buzz and a spark of light on the horizon. Some young, lively machines ripped through the sky with a clean, hissing sound like someone cutting a piece of satin with a knife; there were also ominous, dark airplanes that rooted around above us as if they were looking for the right place to drop their bombs. They all crossed the sky incessantly, day and night, untouchable, powerful creatures that watched over our actions from high up, impossible beings capable of flying even though they were made of iron.

"Here they come; here they come," Grandmother would say.

And I never found out if she was referring to the airplanes or those birds who she alone could see. Grandmother Barbara was very odd; sometimes she had a fever, and sometimes she was as cold as ice. A young doctor who came to see her scratched his head, embarrassed, and confessed that he couldn't find anything wrong with her. But Grandmother continued to shrivel up a little more each day.

"The shadows in this house are to blame; they've made us all turn inward," Airelai declared.

And she must have been right, because since the Great Fire, the world seemed much more unpleasant. The sun showed up hesitantly over our gloomy hole of a courtyard and never ventured to come in. During the day, the light in our rooms was gray and heavy like dusk; it crept along the floor of the rooms, distributing shadows to all the corners. In the dwarf woman's room, that is in the dressing room downstairs, there weren't even windows.

One afternoon when both Airelai and Segundo were gone, it occurred to me to go down to explore the dressing room. I didn't think I would find anything special there; I was just bored. Grandmother was dozing off, Amanda was preparing dinner, and Chico had gone under the kitchen table, like he often did, to be as close as possible to his mother. At the boarding house, when I didn't know what to do to kill the time, I went to the dwarf woman's room to snoop around in her boxes and coffers. I liked to look at the sparkle of her costumes and smell and caress armfuls of soft muslin that were in her large trunks. Airelai's perfume—a striking mossy, damp forest scent—had saturated her entire wardrobe.

when I went down to the dressing room that afternoon, it was the first time that I ventured alone into the dwarf woman's room after the Great Fire. Even though I knew that the chests had been saved from the fire, I was still surprised to find that everything was intact and that something from the old world lived on in this one. What moved me the most was being able to see the dwarf woman's trunk bed again. I lifted the top carefully, and it was all there: the bed delicately finished with embroidered sheets, the silk pillow, the crimson lining decorated with postcards—the whale emerging from frothy water; the tiny, meticulous colored drawing of the Hindu gods; the photo of a stone cabin in the mountains; the little, old woman standing up on a table; the dazzling portrait of the Star.

I kept looking at these cards for a long time trying to remember how I'd pondered them the first time and what I'd felt when I discovered them, before I knew all about them. But one can never fully remember being innocent—that is, being ignorant. Now it seems unbelievable to me that there was ever a time when I was unaware of the Star's existence. How did I manage to live without being sure, like I was now, of happiness' inevitable arrival? I sighed and plunged my finger into the lace pillow; it was soft and smooth. Next, with the same finger, I felt the mattress, which was much firmer. Without stopping to think, going on impulse, I took off my shoes and put one leg into the trunk. Then I stopped to think, and I put the other one in. I'd always wanted to know how it felt inside the reddish, satin shelter that seemed so comfortable. I sat on the bed, and then I lay down. The trunk was small for me, and I had to keep my knees bent a little, but even so, it was pleasant. I stretched my hand and closed the curved top over me. It didn't fit completely because the lock's metal latch was in the way, leaving a gap of about a centimeter around the edge. Light slipped inside through that space. Outside, in the dressing room light came from an ugly neon tube attached to the ceiling; it was pallid and disheartening. But sliding through the gap of the lid, that dull light bounced around the cherry-red silk lining, and the inside was colored by a warm, pink hue with a fleshy, sweet quality. I sighed and mumbled my talisman word, baba-baba-baba, feeling better than I had in a long time. The lace on the pillow brushed my ears, and I was a dwarf woman—small, very smal—and I knew that nothing bad could happen to me while I stayed inside that circular half-light, inside that warm, nourishing air.

Then, I heard some steps in the room. It was someone noisy and tall; it couldn't have been Airelai. I fidgeted inside the trunk trying not to make noise until I could peep through the crack. It was Segundo, as I feared, and having him so close, cruel and glowering, froze my blood. I saw him shove chests aside to open a closet and then empty it of spotlights, tools, boxes with cables. He took out the empty shelves then, and finally struck the back wall of the closet, opening a small hole, from which he removed a blue suitcase. He put it on top of the dressing table, dug through the locks with a key, and made the two latches spring open at the same time. It was full of money. The suitcase was full of bills—lots and lots of bills, like the ones the dwarf woman brought home when she went out at night. This had to be what Portuguese and the Shark were after when they came to our house.

Segundo carefully took out the wads and when the suitcase was empty, he reached inside and took out a panel, which served as a false bottom. Under the panel there was something thin and rectangular that looked like a chocolate bar, only it was blue in color and appeared sticky. Segundo grabbed the bar and, with the help of a screwdriver, he hooked some cables and some dark pieces to the bluish plastic and then screwed it all onto the suitcase with great care. He covered the device with the false bottom and filled it with the wads of bills; then, he closed the top and the latches, and then he had to repeat his earlier efforts in reverse order and lug all the packages, the cables, the spotlights and coffers from here to there until he could leave the suitcase hidden in the secret bowels of the closet. Segundo was sweating profusely after all that effort. I gazed at is his fat, reddened face, his brutal scar through the gap from my hiding place. And I, too, found myself drenched in a cold sweat; his maneuvers had taken some time and my body was cramped, and my nerves were on edge.

He turned halfway and started toward the door, but as he passed by the trunk, he tripped on my shoes. He took a few steps back and swore while I felt like I was dying inside my tomb. But then he regained his balance and kicked the sandals out of his way without paying much attention to them, believing perhaps that they were Airelai's. He finally left the dressing room furiously. It took a long time for me to dare to get out of the trunk, and when I did, my arms were trembling so much that I could barely lift the lid.

Segundo had always been a man who was difficult to deal with, but now, since his return, his mood was darker than ever and his wishes more unpredictable. Now he was nervous and stressed, as if waiting for something. Like an animal who fears being hunted. At the same time, nevertheless, he seemed more sure of himself. He dared to shout at Grandmother Barbara, forcing her out of her small bed. Without a doubt, he now governed the house—with orders that were always contradictory. He mixed cruel force with suspicion, and arrogance with worry; as we were not used to this new twist in character, we didn't know how to protect ourselves or hide ourselves from his sudden rages.

His presence became so exhausting that Airelai decided to use magic against him. The dwarf woman would admit that she lacked power against Segundo. That they knew each other too well, and that the man had inherited insurmountable shields against her spells from his father. But one afternoon, she explained to us that there is a power that all women have even if they don't know it, which is the power of movement between life and death, the power of blood and of silence, just like there is a power that men have although they may have no idea about it, which is the power of rust and iron, the power of force and territory. Therefore, all women who are the right age can exercise an enchanting influence, as long as they know the correct methods. Airelai concluded that it must be Amanda, who, with her help, would bewitch Segundo.

Amanda was not very sure if she was capable of doing it because she was never sure of anything. She didn't know if she believed in spells, but she didn't know if she disbelieved them either. Above all, she doubted herself and her ability to achieve a better life. She distrusted fate so much that she thought that all changes were for the worse, like the way her own life happened; it had been bad as a girl, worse as a teenager, much worse when she became Segundo's girlfriend, disastrous after the wedding, and was approaching catastrophe at this moment. Her? Power? It wasn't possible, Amanda rejected the thought, blindly opening and closing her round eyes repeatedly.

Then the dwarf woman began to tell her stories of the innate strength of women, how they steam up mirrors when they appear as menstruating females, or how plants wither, cats' hair stands on end, sick children sleep calmly, sauces curdle, light bulbs burn out, apples become rotten, wounds heal, and compotes become moldy if a woman who is bleeding touches them.

"And what's more," Airelai said finally, "if you put as much effort into the spell as you are putting into saying no, it will surely come out wonderfully."

And then Amanda smiled, and her pale cheeks became rosy, and she nodded her head in agreement.

The dwarf woman explained that it was to be a very simple spell that was common in the towns in the south, where she had learned it. It was called the seasoning charm whereby a woman seasoned people by a dose of her menstrual fluid. Putting a few drops of blood in a cup of coffee was enough. The victim had to drink it without noticing anything, and his will immediately became weak, as the people from the south would say, which is, trapped by and subordinate to the menstruating woman.

"I have never been able to confirm this spell personally, because as you know, there is no monthly cycle in my womb," Airelai concluded. "But I understand that it is very effective, above all if it is used against a man and if the victim is the husband or lover of the woman who performs the act. We should try it; we have nothing to lose."

And that's how it was; they waited until Amanda's next period, and they laced one of the countless glasses of cognac that Segundo drank with a few drops. The man swallowed the glassful and then two or three more, which were now free of blood, and although he didn't notice anything odd about his drink, his behavior didn't seem to change either. He went to bed as violent and drunk as he did every night.

A few days later, it became evident that the spell didn't have the least effect. Segundo had not only not become weak, but he seemed even more irate and demented. He came and went, slamming the doors loudly; he locked himself in the empty dressing room for hours, where I imagined him taking out the suitcase and putting it away, counting and recounting the money. Dark circles were growing around his eyes, and one night he interrupted the magic show and punched one of the customers.

"I told you I was no good at this," Amanda complained.

"It's that you girls today are different," the dwarf woman pondered. "The old customs don't work anymore; the traditional spells are of no use. It's strange—your blood no longer causes wilting, nor does it heal. You're mutant beings."

So everything went on as normal after the magic's failure; with Grandmother shrinking more and more and Segundo becoming larger and larger.

"Listen to the birds. Listen to the wretched birds," Grandmother Barbara would say once in awhile.

But they were still only planes, roaring over our heads paying no attention to us. Just like the sun, which almost never showed up in our courtyard now. The summer was marching toward its end; the days were getting shorter, and our apartment was a damp, shadowy hole. Amanda and Airelai devised the idea of pushing Grandmother's little bed next to the window; they opened the pane, put two pillows on the windowsill, and since the temperature was still warm and nice, they laid Grandmother down with her head outside on top of the pillows so that she could gaze up above everything—through the mouth of the courtyard, at the tiny, brilliant, blue square of unattainable sky. Once in a while a plane would cross through that clear box, and Grandmother Barbara, without a word, would point at it with a melancholy finger.

CHAPTER TWENTY-TWO

Grandmother Barbara was getting worse. Her hands trembled, and her head had become full of thoughts as dark as her eyes. One day, for example, she insisted on celebrating her death day. She woke up very early and called the dwarf woman and Amanda, and she forced them to buy a cake and make a pitcher of thick, hot chocolate.

Airelai decorated Grandmother's room with little paper lanterns and streamers, and she hung a ribbon of cheap lace, like the kind they sell at flea markets, around the bed. That was Grandmother's idea, who said that the lace was a very apt adornment because it was reminiscent of the border around death announcements. When everything was ready, we had the celebration. We blew out the single candle on the cake, and we ate it. It was very good as was the hot chocolate that Amanda had prepared. Chico and I lit sparklers; their tiny fires fell sweetly on our hands without burning us.

"It was a lovely death day," Grandmother said with a very tired voice. "I would like to have guessed correctly. I would like to die on a day like today a year from now."

"What morbid thoughts!" Airelai protested shuddering.

Grandmother furrowed her brow; I could see that the comment had bothered her. She got up on one elbow with some effort, her eyes gleaming again with black light. "What do you know! What do you know! I only want one more year. That is all I ask for. I wish I could have one year! And don't be so sure of yourself; perhaps this is my death day, but it could possibly be yours. Because we all have one – that dark hour waits for us all... even her," she said turning toward me; she was speaking furiously, as if she were angry with me. "Even girls like you become old and die."

She was panting and, exhausted, let herself fall onto the bed. Chico and I began to laugh because Grandmother no longer induced fear, and now it was funny when she got irritated. So we laughed with our arms crossed and the sparklers filling our hands with stars. That is how the last party ended.

After that day Grandmother Barbara got much worse. She barely spoke; she spent her hours gazing at that rectangle of sky and dozing. Once in a while she whispered, "Water."

And she stated it with great refinement and feeling, like someone saying the name of a loved one. The first few times Amanda gave her something to drink, but that wasn't what she was talking about.

"If we could only take her to the sea or at least to a lake," the dwarf woman surmised.

But they had closed the park again, shortly after its grand opening, and the Neighborhood was hundreds of kilometers from the nearest coast. One day Airelai constructed a cross with some large wooden matches, and then lit it on fire. It was, she explained, a hex against the burning air and the feverish earth, a spell for water and moisture. In fact, shortly after the cross was consumed, it began to rain. The next day—and this was the important part— three or four workers with their large machines appeared and began to take out the pavement in the tiny square at the top of our street.

"They're making a fountain, a beautiful fountain," Chico came to tell us breathlessly as soon as he found out.

The jack hammer sounded like a machine gun, and the excavator like a tank, and together the clamor was so tremendous, it seemed like a war had broken out just a few meters from the house. The planes could no longer be heard, and the earth was shaking such that your teeth were chattering on the glass when you tried to drink water. We began to think that this time the dwarf woman had gone too far with her spell. But the work was hurried; in a few days they had already made a huge hole, and then they covered it with cement and smoothed it. One morning we woke up in the middle of a deathly silence, almost deafening because it was so rare. We went down to see what was happening and discovered that the workers had disappeared with all their greasy smoking machines, even though the fountain didn't seem to be finished. Instead of a fountain, it seemed to be more like a shallow, circular pond; it had a simple cement ledge and it was covered by a few inches of black water. In the center, there was a square, cement base from which some already rusty re-bar jutted out, along with some plastic pipes. A few meters from the fountain, leaning against the wall in a pile of rubble, there was a rudimentary stone fish with its wide open mouth that was probably destined to go over the cement base.

We waited a few days to see if the workers would come back, but the fountain was still abandoned. The fish lost its fins after having stones thrown at it, and now it looked like a highway signpost with eyes. As for the water, it was thick and dirty, brimming with cans and garbage. A little stray dog drank two big laps and lurched away with all sorts of difficulty, like a drunk. Not even the stupidest bird dared to look at his reflection in the surface. But there was no other water nearby, and we were pressed for time. So one afternoon, we dressed Grandmother in one of the two outfits Segundo had bought her after the fire—it was dark, sad clothing for an elderly woman and very different from the fine dresses that she had before. And we went down with Grandmother Barbara to see the pond.

She didn't say anything, but I know she liked it. Some afternoons, when she had enough strength, she asked me to accompany her to the fountain. The trough became more and more vile, and it even reeked, but it seemed like Grandmother must have been looking at something else when she looked at the stagnant water. Grandmother Barbara's eyes were beginning to be covered with a blue film, like newborns' eyes. She was now capable of fixing her misty look on an object and keeping it still for a long time without even blinking. In that way, undaunted and statuesque, Grandmother Barbara gazed at the surface of the fountain at dusk while I, who was bored, counted the squashed beer cans, the tattered papers, and scraps of plastic that were floating in the puddle. She must have recognized the sun's liquid reflection from her memory—that golden spark that slid lazily along the gelatinous, dirty, black surface of the putrid water despite everything.

CHAPTER TWENTY-THREE

Chico was gone for a day and a half when he ran away. He didn't talk a lot, he took care of his odd jobs, sat in the sun or shade on the stoop, and watched life pass without making many moves. Sometimes he seemed like a fool, and generally he didn't seem like anything; I mean to say that you didn't stop to look at him or think twice about him. But I knew he wasn't stupid and that he had the memory of an elephant. I was growing, and that summer I hit such a serious growth spurt that my eyes were now above the frame of the mirror at the club. But Chico was still the same as he always was, and I was leaving him behind – he was just about up to the last of my ribs. I think that he used up all his energy with his memory, and that's why he didn't grow. For example, he learned cars' license plates by heart to know if new people were coming around the Neighborhood. He knew when each neighbor came and went, their usual routes, their schedules and how things unfolded with their routines.

He behaved that way because he felt the need to know and control everything, for any change, no matter how small, terrified him. That's why his escape turned out to be so extraordinary for him, even heroic. Undoubtedly, the cause that forced him to leave had to be very powerful, but he never told us why he did it. Nevertheless, one afternoon, after I'd softened him up with a gift of a few licorice sticks and half a bar of white chocolate, which was his weakness, Chico told me, if not the reason for his flight, what happened during that day and a half.

"What frightened me the most was leaving our area. Because I am the king here, I mean, king of the children. I know where to go, who to greet, and who to avoid. Since I know so many things, I'm stronger than you here, even though you don't know it, and I am stronger about other things because you don't know; I don't know if you get it. Though I don't want you to understand me too well, so you won't learn too much. Because you're taller and older, and Grandmother loves you more, so it's fair that you know less than I do so that things are even. But I was saying that at first what scared me the most was leaving our area and meeting other bosses, because on all the corners in the Neighborhood, there is some boss, or that is, everyone has someone to fear. It's just that some fear many, and others only fear a few, and I am afraid of everyone except for my mother and perhaps you. Well, not you either.

"The thing that occurred to me is that I had to find some excuse to cross into the other areas in the Neighborhood without anything bad happening to me. The idea was to be something beyond what I am in my corner because I already told you that you can be more or less safe within the Neighborhood if you know your place and you don't leave your territory. That day that I ran away from home, I immediately thought about business because merchants tend to defend their interests with great enthusiasm, so I thought they could protect me at least a little bit. And so, I began to traverse the Neighborhood going from shop to shop, as if I were on an errand to buy something. I walked very decisively and with certainty with my eyes fixed on the next shop that appeared on the horizon, and people looked at me and thought I was a customer and left me alone.

"The most difficult part was when I was in front of the stores; generally, I stopped to look at the display, pretended for a while, and then I moved on toward the next shop. Sometimes there were some suspicious kids around, and I felt obligated to enter the premises, although the shopkeepers could be worse than the kids, and there was one who slapped me as he threw me out of his grocery because he thought that I was stealing from him. Of course the advantage kids have over shopkeepers was that the shopkeepers never afford to get far from their own store, and if you leave running, they won't follow you.

"The plan worked like a charm, and I crossed through the Neighborhood in a few hours. I was so happy with my success that I tried to add a finishing touch, and I began to make a few bottle caps jingle in my hand as if they were coins that I was going to use for my purchase. That turned out to be a mistake because a boy grabbed me on a corner, cuffed me twice, and took my money. After seeing that it wasn't money but bottle caps, he clobbered me a little more. That was when my t-shirt, face, and neck got stained with blood. And even though it hurt, it wasn't that bad because after that, I came up with a new plan to keep walking, and it was this: every time I saw a gang or someone suspicious, I started to weave and stumble along as if I were about to faint, and then everyone moved out of the way and let me by as if I would were contagious. You already know that it's best that no one sees you in the Neighborhood, but if they see you, then the best is for them to see you a lot. I'm saying that if you attract a lot of attention, they'll avoid you, too, and I was attracting a lot of attention with blood all over me and by walking that way.

"So I walked for a good, long time, and I was already dying of hunger, despite the apples that I had taken from the market, and I arrived at the edge of the Neighborhood, at a large, dry park, where if you cross to the other side, the Lovely City begins. I entered the park and washed the blood off my face in a fountain because I thought that attracting attention was no longer good. The park was full of kids. It was the afternoon, and I saw a girl sitting on rock making faces at her sandwich. She was a very thin girl with skinned knees, and I sat next to her, and we started to talk. She said her mother was forcing her to eat that disgusting bologna sandwich full of black bits that were very spicy, and it was true that her mother was looking at us sternly from the bench across from us, with a furious expression. I told her that if she wanted, I could pretend to steal the sandwich from her, and she said yes, that that was marvelous. Then I explained that she had to look the other way and hold the bread loosely with her fingers. The girl did that, and I took a shot at the sandwich and left running; I heard the mother's screams at my back, but she couldn't catch me of course. I ate the bologna, and it tasted great to me.

"Finally, I arrived at a station, which is where I wanted to get to, because I had thought about leaving the city, even though I hadn't decided how I was going to board the train. There were a lot of people, fast legs that took strides one way or another in the lobby, suitcases and purses, carts and packages. I was tired, very tired, and I thought it would be good to sleep for a little while. So I took advantage of the stir and entered the restroom. I went into one of the stalls, locked the door, and laid down on the floor curled up against the wall next to the toilet. I fell asleep right away, and I woke up—I'm not sure how much later—with a huge face very close to mine, and a huge, tough hand that was shaking me. It was a great scare because I had come face to face with a police officer; he whisked me through the air and out of the restroom. He was a very tall guard, with a ferocious face, who was shouting things I didn't understand. A woman officer came right away with a blanket and wrapped me in her arms, and I liked that better.

"We left the station; I was wrapped in the blanket, holding the uniformed woman's hand. Outside the sky was black, and the city was empty. It had to be very late, later than it had ever been my whole life, except for the nights of the festival and the Great Fire, and for the first time, I was happy that the guards were close by. We got into a police car—you should have seen it—all new with a dashboard full of lights, and we went to the police station, and they gave me chocolate milk and cookies and a bed. But despite how weary I felt, I couldn't get to sleep because everything was exciting, and I was thinking it was a pain to be so small, and that's why they had brought me in.

"I want to grow, you know, I want to grow right away, as soon as possible. And when I grow, I won't be like my mother, no, because Mom isn't in charge of anything. And I don't want to be like my father because Dad wouldn't let me be like him. He would kill me if he thought that I was going to be like him and that I would take his place. And I don't want to be like the dwarf woman either because I don't understand her. I don't have imagination because I don't have time for that, and besides, one day I saw how the kids in the Neighborhood were throwing stones at her, and she may very well be a powerful witch, but she did nothing more than run, and since she is so small, she could barely run. So I have decided that I'm going to be like Grandmother, but like Grandmother before the Great Fire, when she was tall and she gave so many orders, like when she took out that pistol with Portuguese and the Shark. Of course, it seems to me that the thing about being a grandmother is not a profession, I mean that you have to do something more to earn a living. I'm good at pretending, so I think that I can be an actor, and I can also be a merchant, because I like business a lot. But the best thing I have is my memory, and since I pay attention so much and I know everyone, I think it would go very well for me as a blackmailer, like they say Rita's husband is, which is an occupation that brings in a lot of money, and if you don't think so, notice the kind of shop Rita has. I'm telling you this, but don't tell anyone because it's still a secret.

"The thing is that thinking about all this, I shouldn't have fallen asleep at the police station, but I remember that someone woke me up again, and now it was daytime. They gave me chocolate milk again and more cookies, and a man who they said was a doctor came to see me, and a new man and woman who asked me things. I lied to them very politely and told them that I didn't remember my last name, and that I didn't know where I lived or how I had gotten lost. About my torn eyebrow and the blood on my shirt, I told them that I had stumbled and fallen. They asked me about the scars from my old blows, and I told them that a very bad boy named Buga had hit me, because since he is dead, I thought mentioning him wouldn't matter, and it's always good to give them one name to keep them happy. Then they put me in the car again and brought me home, you saw it. The whole time they insisted on asking me the same question about how they treated me at home. I always answered that my mom and my dad loved me a lot, because the police go away, but parents stay. Even fathers who leave always come back."

CHAPTER TWENTY-FOUR

When we moved to the new apartment after the Great Fire, Grandmother's small bed was so tight for her that her hips and shoulders hung over both sides. But with time, the bed became loose around her body, like outfits become loose on obese men who become sick and get thin. Grandmother Barbara had shriveled so much that now she barely made the sheet bulge, and only in the middle. It wasn't because she had lost a few pounds, but rather that even the parts of her body that couldn't possibly shrink, had shrunk—like her hands, which were huge dominating hands with fearful fists before and were just a heap of bones now, translucent little spiders walking clumsily and slowly along the covers.

Sometimes she lost her voice, or perhaps she found herself so weak that she didn't have the strength to exhale, and then she pointed toward herself with her wiry hand, and with gestures, she asked us to move her a little or push her, or rock her like one rock's a child in order to cool her from the sheets' burning. She had bedsores and limbs like the dead, and inside all that ruin, her entire intelligence was boiling. She, who always got so dressed up and who was so concerned about her appearance, suffered the humiliation of having a dirty, broken corpse beyond her control. She was a prisoner inside her own body, a passenger, dragged by her biological journey, and she continued to wait, besieged by the pain and by the death of everything.

On the other hand, she was still like a marble sculpture sometimes, and she gathered all her energy to pull out an almost inaudible trickle of a voice, "What's the weather outside," she asked without any intonation or questioning because she didn't have enough breath for that.

"It's nice," responded the afflicted Amanda, who like her son didn't have an imagination either.

"What's the weather outside," Grandmother Barbara would repeat as if she had not heard.

And then Airelai, who guessed what Grandmother wanted, would describe life and the way things were on the other side of the window and outside of death's torrential and undaunted throes:.

"Today is a very clear day because the wind came and took all that remained of the month of August away. In place of those dusty remnants of summer, that were dragging through the streets up until yesterday, a transparent air that smells a bit like winter has entered the world. It is an extremely fine air, and I fear that it will take its leave soon. But today it is delicious to feel its cool brush on your cheeks and to soak it in through your lips. It tastes like a drop of rain."

And Grandmother Barbara fixed her misty eyes on the ceiling and savored her memories of fall, which were a part of her secret, intimate luggage that she would take with her.

On occasions Grandmother suffered from attacks in which the bit of breath that she still had seemed to want to flee the ruin of her skin and bones. Then she tensed up and clung, with her glass fingers, to the headboard, which was a curved bar with many blemishes in its nickel-plating. And like that – grabbing onto the world so that the world would not leave, with her eyes like two terrified wells, fighting against the black anguish—she would begin to recite a monotonous mantra.

"I am Barbara Mondragon Salva Jimenez Darsena ... I am Barbara Mondragon Salva Jimenez Darsena ..."

She repeated her name over and over again so she wouldn't forget herself, so that she wouldn't become diffused in the darkness that was waiting for her, as if she preferred that agony of horror and pain to a nothingness that was perhaps sweet and devoid of memory.

"What's the weather outside..."

"A dry storm. Lightening is flashing through the sky, but not even a drop of rain is falling here below. Well yes, there is a light wind that lifts up little clouds of dust and scratches your legs. It is a strange day, and the air is yellow."

Airelai was lying because the afternoon was clear, gray, and insipid. But the changes in the seasons didn't show up on our courtyard, so it was neither here nor there to say one thing or another.

"But why are you here with her? Why do you treat her so well?" Amanda asked the dwarf woman one morning, whispering, while Grandmother dozed for a little while.

"And you?"

"For the usual reasons. It's my duty."

"Why?"

"Who is going to do it if I don't? It's my destiny."

"Why?"

"Oh, why, why?... I have bad luck – you already know about it. That's how things are. But you... You're not obligated. Plus, she wasn't good to you either."

"Nor was I at times."

"I mean that it was difficult to love her."

"We have been together many years. She is part of my life. I know her well, and she understands me. Sometimes knowing is more binding than affection."

"I wish I hadn't known her. Not her, or her son."

"That's the way life is. Why bother dreaming that things had been different? Wishes for the future do enough harm already— on top of that, why torture yourself with stupid wishes about the past? But you asked me why I am here, and I'm going to give you an answer: to see how death is, to keep learning."

Grandmother was going up the last hill of her life laboriously, and her chest sounded like a bellows full of cracks. It seemed unreal that a being that was so tiny and fragile could make that noise without breaking. Segundo began to come into her room from time to time. His somber face appeared, with its stubble, and he wore a dirty shirt because now he had let himself go, he didn't get dressed up like before. He would stick his face in, and he scrunched up his mug because, even though we kept the window open, the air in the room was sour and thick. He finally took a few steps forward and leaned over Grandmother's bed, looked, and was quiet without making a single gesture. He seemed like a hyena waiting for the last breath, in order to sink his teeth in.

"What's the weather outside..."

"It's snowing," lied the dwarf woman. "It's a gloomy, brilliant day, no wind, and the snowflakes fall very slowly. Everything is white, soft, and very lovely. And there is a silence and a peace in the air that invite sleep."

But Grandmother Barbara clung convulsively to the blemished bedframe and gasped for breath not wanting to lose ground in the battle that would conclude the nightmare of her journey. When her gasps became death rattles, Amanda deemed it time tell Segundo. He entered the room with his head sunk between his shoulders, filling the room with his enormous presence. He sat on the bed, which moaned under his weight. He scrutinized Grandmother Barbara for a few moments, and then—it was extraordinary—he took one of the woman's arachnid hands in his own colossal hands. There those transparent little fingers rested, shaken by minute trembles, cradled delicately and timidly in the claws of Segundo, who observed his mother attentively and with anxiety, as if waiting for something. Some time passed like that, while the minutes slipped away from the afternoon like the last grains of sand slip through an hourglass. Then Grandmother opened her eyes wide, lifted her head a little from the bed, gazed at her son fixedly, and said, "Maximo."

We heard a horrific crunching, the crack of fragile bones breaking when Segundo closed his huge hands over his mother's. But maybe Grandmother Barbara didn't feel anything because when she fell back down on the pillow, she was already dead. Then Segundo stood up and howled. He howled like a crazy person, like a wild animal, with a primal, ferocious sound that bounced on the walls of the room and made our hair stand on end. And when Amanda, the dwarf woman, and I believed that our time had come, and that he would tear us all to pieces to satisfy the hatred that was vibrating in his scream, the man turned, collided with the wall, jerked open the door, wrenching it off the frame, and staggered out of the room.

CHAPTER TWENTY-FIVE

I was afraid of growing too much, of changing so much that when my father came back, he wouldn't be able to recognize me. At the end of that summer, I had another growth spurt, and for a few days, I had to adapt to the new geometry of the world. My eyes were now above the large bolt on the door, whose spotted metal edge I only saw if I was on tiptoes before, and the windows became smaller, and now I had to duck down to see the inside of the wooden cabinet, which had a knot that looked like a tiger's eye.

I was afraid of growing too much, and I also had another, more desperate fear, which was that of having changed irreversibly and having learned too much already because I remembered, among moving shadows, that faraway, ancient innocent time, much earlier than my arrival by train to the city, even before that big gray house where I stayed for some dark years with other sad children, and I believe I saw a blurry tall, blue figure, who was without a doubt my father, and who caressed my face in silence with his warm, blue finger. And my face must have been a different face then because that happened in a distant era, being so small that I wasn't even myself yet. I never doubted my father's return; I knew that one day he would inevitably arrive, the same way that the Star would arrive, our brilliant Star of good times. But I feared he wouldn't remember, that he would pass by without even looking at me, as if he were blind and I were invisible. And sometimes I dreamed it; I dreamt that my father passed through me inadvertently, and I didn't have hands to stop him or a voice to warn him, and I was nothing more than a fistful of transparent air, and he was a blue tree that walked alone.

But sometimes the dwarf woman would tell me not to worry, that when the time came, my father would not have any problem recognizing me, like wolves always recognize the cubs lost from their own litter in the middle of an icy field. And that all those fears are nothing but the fear of waiting itself, ghosts of the absence. She knew it well, she explained, because she also awaited a loved one, and the empty days of waiting fell on her back like drops of molten lead – painfully and slowly. It was on one of those days, after Grandmother's death, when Airelai told us this story:

"I know full well what it is for a man to want you. Many men have wanted me, with a need like fire's that has to keep burning things up in order to survive; and so it burns straw if it's nearby, and if not, wood, or cloth, or cardboard, thorns and brambles, soft plants and ferns, and even little live animals that try to escape its roasting tongue. Fire burns indiscriminately; it devours everything it touches. In that very way, so hungry and blind, some men have wanted to burn me up. But that kind of fire has no power over me; only other flames can catch me.

"Many men have desired me and for different reasons: because I'm a monster and because I'm perfect, because I'm very old or because I look like a girl. They all wanted my body and they took it; some, more savage and cruel than others, also possessed my pain or my fear. But just one man got my will and my time. That man made me his slave, because I loved him and I love him still. And passion is a sickness of the soul that makes you lose your freedom once and for all. Passion cannot exist without slavery; and if you love without that sense of disaster, without that anxious dependence on the one you love, then you just don't love him truly. Love is nature's strongest drug and the most perverse; it's a brilliant evil that tricks you with its colored sparks, while it devours you. But once you've lived that feverish passion, you can't let yourself go back to the dismal life of living sensibly.

"When I met him he was good to me, which says a lot, because those were hard times full of crude people. He had enormous, bony hands that never left a trace on me; unlike his breath, which engraved his initials on my soul. For us Lilliputians, just a small soul can fit in our bodies. He never desired me as blindly and voraciously as fire does; he was there with me, he talked with me, he listened to me. He looked at me as if my eyes were at the same height as his: he is the only man who ever looked at me that way. We went together for many years; I worked with him, lived with him, we shared everything except a bed. But it didn't matter too much to me that that part of our relationship was missing, the element that slightly scrupulous fires had scorched. If we were together—and we were together many hours of the day—I felt satisfied.

"But one day something went wrong, and he was obliged to flee at once. I saw him pack his suitcase hurriedly, sure of losing him. Tears ran down my face and I didn't bother to hide them because I was sure that, in his excitement, he wouldn't even have time to look at me. And then something marvelous happened, the most beautiful thing that had ever happened to me in my whole life: he turned around, he gazed at me from his unreachable height and exclaimed, 'But aren't you ready yet?'

"I have recalled that moment so many times now that his face is fading on me, worn out by remembering it. But I still see his profile, the shadow of his body bending over me, the gleam in his eyes between foggy features, and I still feel that fiery tongue, the flash that ran down my back when I heard his words, a lightning bolt of pure and complete happiness. I think that I levitated, I floated, and the Caravacan cross on the roof of my mouth surely became incandescent. Today, so many years later, my eyes still sting foolishly when I remember it.

"We traveled through, or more accurately, we were on the run through most of the country, never spending two nights in the same place; and in the end we pulled into a good hideout, a run-down stone cabin in a remote valley. We stayed there and we were content.

"You two are still very young and don't know what it's like to have your life at your back, like a messy bag of leftovers—treasures and trash all mixed up, a bundle that keeps growing as it hangs over your shoulder and weighs you down more and more each day. Recollections are fused onto your memory, past years, fulfilled and unfulfilled desires, dreams and tears; the scenes of yesterday lose all of life's light and rhythm. They are melted into a gray conglomeration of confusing, dusty, and faraway images that you might say had been lived by some other person and not by you. It's as if someone were walking in the country and crossed a valley and climbed a hill; and she looks back and notices that the valley that she has just crossed is filled with shadows, and she can no longer make out the path that she followed through the landscape, which is just now brimming with the night. Because the hollys that were shining so brightly in the sun before, have lost their luster now, the flowers have no color anymore, the river no longer glimmers, the switchbacks of that same path are just barely distinguishable in the obscurity. The fact is that the night that waits for us is also devouring the footprints left by our steps.

"But there are times, moments in your life that remain glistening in your memory even though time has passed; and when you look back you see that memory blazing in the shapeless grayness of the past, like an island of light in a pool of shadows. That's how the days that I spent with him in that cabin burn in my mind; it's a fire that blinds me when I look back, a brilliance that hurts. Among the shadows of my life, those days still keep glowing.

"It was an exquisite valley; it was nearly abandoned with just a few stone and slate houses. An old, damp forest stretched along the hillsides, with centuries-old oaks, knobby and covered with mushrooms and lichen. There were lush chestnut trees with spiny fruit, prickly hollys, and soft, silky ferns like peacock feathers. The ground was as cushiony as a mattress, with layers of dead leaves, mulch, roots, fungi, microscopic organisms, busy insects, and critters of all shapes and sizes. Everything was crackling, rustling, and decaying, driven by life's unstoppable force. And the air smelled like freshly cut hay, like juicy moss, like cattle, like thick decomposing earth.

"We both knew that it wouldn't last. We were fugitives in our last hideout. I felt as if I were condemned to death, as we all are really, waiting for my happiness to end—because it always comes to an end. But in the meantime I drank the days, hours, and minutes greedily, feeling the wind of time pass right over my face.

"There was an orchard near our little house; it was owned by the man who rented us our cabin. Every day his daughter, a girl about ten or eleven years old, went there. She spent her hours sitting next to a beautiful fig tree, singing one song after another to scare the birds away so they wouldn't eat the fleshy figs. I listened to her sing, when the sun shined and during the heat, while the flies buzzed and the hills boiled, while he slept for a while in that rickety old bed. I watched him as he slept; he was so beautiful and mine when he was still, and I knew that I would never be able to live anything better.

"At those moments, the world acquired a perfect geometry, a visible order that I felt I could understand. I felt at home, in that exact place in the universe that belonged to me, and all the rest of the planet's creatures were in their right places as well. I could see and understand everything in that moment of balance: the infinite leaves in the valley, each and every one, even the smallest; the worn rocks, buried in the flesh of the earth: every single unique flower, trembling during its short life; the tiny insects' legs, their transparent wings, their sucking stingers; and that tumult of budding flowers and wilting petals, of creatures being born and dying, between death's fruitful wind and life's silent howling.

"Until that time came to an end, as it always inevitably does. They came to the valley; they found us and took him away. But I know that he'll come back someday, and I'm waiting for him here. I would do anything for him: kill, betray, lie, even deny myself. I was always awkward, except with him. I was always weak, except with him. I was always a dwarf, but not to him. Ever since he left, my life has just been a time of waiting. An in-between time. A dead time.

"I remember that at dusk, the clamor of animals' bellows and shrieks would blow our way in the wind from the opposite hillside. We often stayed there contemplating the sunset, while the air was painted a bluish green color, and the animals' wild voices came to us echoing through the valley. I always thought they were mating calls, moans of heat and pleasure. But then, after they discovered our hideout and took him away, I found out that the uproar was coming from a slaughterhouse, and they were screams of agony torn from the butcher's knife. From then on, every time I think of those last twilight hours, I see them in my memory in the color of blood: beautiful, transparent, and terrible. That's how close sweetness is to horror, in this life that is so dark and beautiful."

CHAPTER TWENTY-SIX

The dwarf woman opened the narrow window in Grandmother Barbara's room wide open while Amanda, who was something between disconcerted and full of dread, gazed at Grandmother's corpse, her hands rising and falling in the air as if they were short circuited halfway from her lap to her mouth. I stayed in the corner, camouflaged by my stillness and silence, because I was sure that if they noticed me they would throw me out of the room. I didn't like to be near the corpse, but I liked the idea of leaving less, where that terrorizing, howling Segundo must be crouched down in some corner.

"What are we going to do now?" stammered Amanda, choked up.

"What do you think? She'll have to be laid out."

"No... I mean with ... With him. It's like he's crazy."

The dwarf woman hoisted herself up onto the chair, and she stayed there a while seated, thinking and swinging her feet in the air.

"Well you should go. Look for a job, take the boy, and leave."

"I can't."

"Yes. You can."

"He would kill us."

The dwarf woman sighed and rubbed the palms of her hands on her tiny skirt.

"Don't start that again. Listen, I'll go back to working at night. I'll give you enough money to go far away. So that you can cross the border. That way you'll be safe."

"You would do that for me?"

"I get sick of seeing you so intimidated and heartbroken all the time. Of course I'll do it. For me, not for you."

Airelai got down from the chair with a little jump, she went to the dresser, took out a bottle of rubbing alcohol and a box of gauze.

"Bring some clean sheets for the shroud."

With agility, certainty, and silence, the dwarf woman closed Grandmother's mouth and held her chin tight with a tie, knowing the procedures, expert in performing the last rituals.

"But not those, woman!" she grunted toward Amanda, who brought a cheap set of flowered sheets in hand. "They have to be white."

"Why?"

"Because they do; that's obvious."

"How do you know all these things?"

"How is it that you don't know them? Where do you come from that you have no idea about all this? Basic knowledge, rudimentary understandings that simple women have."

"No one explained it to me..."

"You are a mutant, Amanda. I already told you. You're in no

man's land. What you've lost is lost, and what you've won, you don't even know that you're winning. I hope that when you leave, you wise up a little."

"And the girl? I can't leave her here alone with him. I'll take her with me."

My heart jumped. I wanted to live with Amanda and Chico, but I couldn't leave. I clenched my fists and felt the sharp edge of my nails against my palms. I couldn't. Baba.

"The girl has to stay here, waiting for her father," the dwarf woman said slowly. "I'll take care of her because I'm waiting too."

And then she turned toward me and looked at me with those little impenetrable, black and glossy eyes, that were now much lower than the line of mine, and she looked at me for a few moments and furrowed her brow as if she saw something she didn't like.

"Leave the room," she said finally in a whisper.

"Airelai, please..."

"We have to wash her. Go."

I left the room, and the rest of the house was dark—night was falling, and no one had bothered to turn on a light. I listened for a few moments in silence, as frightened as an animal that waits in the underbrush for the hunter to come down on him. I seemed to hear a hoarse panting that was coming from the kitchen, so I crossed the narrow hall on tiptoes and went into my room. I looked under the bed first, and just like I expected, I found Chico there, glistening with beads of sweat and wrapped in dust balls and shadows.

"What's he doing?" The boy whispered in gasps.

"Who?" I asked, even though I knew.

"Him."

"I don't know. Seems like he's in the kitchen."

Chico came out of his hiding place, crawling on his elbows. He sat on the floor and looked at me with his eyes shining in the darkness.

"What do you think is going to happen now?" he mumbled.

That my father is going to come and save us all. That we'll all live together -- my father, Amanda, the dwarf woman, you, and I – together and happy. That we'll all get out of this place, leave the Neighborhood, and Segundo will stay behind, sitting there in the kitchen forever. I wanted to say that to Chico, but my mouth was dry and I had an iron fist in my stomach, knowing that my father could not take much longer, that he had to return now, before Grandmother disappeared completely. Instead of telling him all that, I shrugged my shoulders vaguely.

"I don't know."

Chico furrowed his brow, and bit his nails nervously. I caressed the cold crystal ball that Grandmother had given to me.

"Baba, baba, baba..."

"What are you saying?"

In my worry, I had betrayed myself. I had said my private word aloud without meaning to.

"Nothing. My stuff." I grumbled.

"What is this 'baba'?" he insisted.

"It's nothing, I tell you. Habit. It doesn't mean anything."

At that moment someone knocked on the door with his knuckles; it was a call that sounded familiar, five raps in a row and then two more. My mouth filled with sour saliva. I stretched my neck and pricked up my ears, waiting. The hall light was turned on, and I heard the dwarf woman's light steps walking to the entrance; the click of the bolt, the growl of the wooden door as it opened. And the voice of a stranger but not acompletely unknown man, "Are you surprised to see me?"

It had to be him; it had to be my father. I stood up and left the room, taking slow steps, because I wanted to run, but at the same time I was afraid; I wanted to get to the door and not get there ever. I went so slowly that Chico went in front of me and got to the foyer before I did. He turned to me with a worried expression.

"It's that police guy," he whispered.

There leaning on the door frame, was the gray haired guy with the dirty shirt who had been talking with Segundo the night of the Great Fire. Chico had found out later he was a captain. I sighed. The guy looked at me for a moment and winked, but he was full of hate.

"We're in mourning," the dwarf woman said. "It's not a good time."

"No?" he smiled. "Well I have to talk to Segundo, and I know he's here."

"I'm telling you that you can't come in. Respect the deceased."

"But friends of the family attend the wake. Isn't that true? I thought you and I were friends..."

He smiled with his mouth but not with his eyes. The dwarf woman clenched her little fists and moved aside. The man entered the house and went straight toward the back as if he knew where he was going, followed by Airelai, Chico and me.

"And the darkness, what is that about?" the guy ridiculed, as he entered the black hole of the kitchen. "Are you hiding or sleeping?"

In the middle of the shadows, next to the table, the darker shape of Segundo was distinguishable. The police officer stretched out his arm and flipped the light switch. The naked bulb on the ceiling lit up above our heads like a dirty, dying sun, the wretched sun of Judgment Day. Segundo blinked, blinded. His eyes were puffy, and his face was swollen with a tormented expression I had never seen on him before. He was rubbing his mouth vigorously with the back of his hand as if he were dirty, or as if the shadows had remained glued to his mug; next, he squeezed his knuckles and made them crack in a horrific way, almost with the same dry, cracked sound with which he had broken his mother's fingers. Then he stretched his huge, heavy, sluggish hands over the table top between potato skins, dirty knives, and bread crumbs. In front of him there was an open, half-empty bottle of cognac.

The police officer clicked his tongue with satisfaction as if he were pleased to see Segundo in a pitiful state. He leaned on the door frame and crossed his arms.

"You should be happier to see me. I came to do you a favor."

Segundo didn't move. He kept his head down and stared like a bull at some indeterminate point on the table.

"I came to tell you something," the man insisted, creating a new, expectant pause.

A couple of seconds crossed the dim kitchen slowly and tic-tic-tick-tocking, slipped under the window while no one moved or said a word.

"Maximo has escaped."

At first I didn't feel any emotion. Perhaps I didn't completely understand the implications of the captain's words. Or perhaps I had already sensed it; I already knew. We all remained still. The man twisted his face, annoyed perhaps by our lack of reaction to the news.

"Let's suppose he comes by here. And if he comes, I'm sure that you won't hesitate to notify us, isn't that right?"

Silence. Without looking, next to me, I noticed Chico's shallow, anxious breathing, like a scared, nervous animal.

"I don't think you'll last long once he arrives," the man added, irritated. "He's better than you."

"It's too late already," the dwarf woman's voice rang out strangely hoarse and tense. "Too late for Grandmother Barbara."

"You're a charming family," snorted the officer. "Don't stop inviting me to birthday parties."

Segundo lifted his head and looked at us with his cloudy eyes. I felt that the captain's body tensed at my side, attentive and waiting. Segundo moved his right hand slowly over the table and grabbed a large knife with a shiny, sharp blade, like a pocketknife. It wasn't an aggressive nor surreptitious movement but rather the lazy, clumsy gesture of someone who was playing with an object. Even so, the officer spread his legs firmly on the floor, seeking better support for an emergency. For a while, Segundo did nothing but give us a dull look, turning the knife over in his hands. Then he lifted it over his head slowly and placed it perpendicular up in the air, pointing down at his left hand, which was still stretched over the table, his palm facing down like a dead person. I took a breath and the knife was still up there, still in the air, pointing threateningly toward his hand. I took another breath and it hadn't moved. But the third time I filled my lungs, I saw the blade come down vertiginously, a lightning bolt of steel drawing through the air. There was a dry thud, and the knife was buried in the back of his hand up to the handle. Someone screamed; perhaps it was me. The shank was so long that it must have been driven into the table, binding his flesh to the wood. Segundo gazed at us calmly, while we tried to regain our speech and our heartbeats. Then he began to pull the handle, and the blade started coming out centimeter by centimeter. It was clean and dazzling, without a drop of blood. The knife came all the way out, and the back of his hand was intact, without any wound; Segundo squeezed the point of the dagger sweetly with his index finger, and the steel retracted with a soft hiss of a well greased spring; it was one of the trick knives from his magic act.

"I knew it was fake; I knew you weren't capable of that," the dwarf woman muttered with an irate voice.

Amanda burst into tears at my back. Segundo sank into the back of the chair and toasted us darkly with the bottle of cognac before taking a big swig.

CHAPTER TWENTY-SEVEN

Often tragedy comes like a flood. One day we believe we are standing firmly on the solid ground of our security, and the next day we discover that our feet are sunk in the muck. Our certainty about the world collapses around us like dominoes until it produces, starting with trivialities, total devastation. That is what Rita, from the shop, told me, only she used other words:

"You see people fall down at your side—this one's husband gets sent to jail, that one gets cancer, that one over there's son dies on her—and you always believe that you have dodged the bullet, because life—I'm telling you that I know a lot about this—is like a war. You think you're safe, I mean, that others are the ones who are plagued, until one day, bam, blood on your leg, and they got you. And when the pain sinks its teeth into you, it won't let you go. Tragedy eats you from head to toe."

She was refilling non-reusable bottles with the help of an ingenious, complicated device, a type of bulky syringe.

"Don't think that these bottles are for me, no, no, no. In my store I like to ensure good quality. This is for Mariano, the guy from the bar by the fountain. He asked me to put cheaper alcohol in the bottles, and I do it because I can and I understand. If you sell it as shots at a bar, you make a tidy little sum. For me, since I usually sell whole bottles, it's not the same. It's not worth it. Besides, on top of that, because then the customers get worked up."

Amanda had sent me to buy some cans of tuna for dinner, and whenever I could, I always dawdled a little at the store because Rita treated me as if I were an adult and always told me interesting things.

"Sometimes tragedy catches you sooner and sometimes later, but it catches you. Think of Amanda, for example. A girl from a good family. And skilled, not like me. But her father died, and her mother couldn't handle her. She didn't tell me about it that way, but I know it must have been that way. And this naïve girl went astray. She was so young when she got involved with that jerk, your uncle. I'm not saying anything—I don't want to—but, what a fool she was. He has a good foundation, I'm not saying he doesn't. But you can see immediately that he's nasty. And a good-for-nothing to boot. He never knew how to do things right; he lacks substance. Your father, on the other hand, he is what I call a man. And a gentleman at that."

To feign disinterest, I moved my finger along the edge of the wooden counter, pretending to concentrate on picking off the chips of old green paint that covered it. I had realized that showing interest in a topic gave adults reason to abandon it immediately. Finally, after a little while, I raised my eyes and saw that Rita had stopped her work, and she was looking at me attentively. She sighed.

"I'm not saying anything else because I don't want to."

She grabbed her syringe and continued on with her endeavor. Above her head the incandescent blue, insect-killing lamp was buzzing.

"Of course, it happens because she lets it. It would never dawn on him to put his hands on me. My Juan is a real brute, but he has laid a hand on me."

She stooped toward me, leaning on the counter, and winked at me, "Plus, I can take him," she whispered and burst into laughter, with her powerful chest and massive arms shaking.

I was jealous of her strength and courage. They stung me, as if someone had passed a finger over the brands on my back, the last lashings Segundo had given me. I looked at my small, weak hands, and I compared them with Rita's bulky hands, which were red and hefty with nails that were so thick they were white.

"Well, I'm going to learn karate," I said.

"Karate?"

"Yes, what they do on TV and in the movies, when they kick and break a door. And you don't have to be big, or even strong. I saw a boy in a movie who beat out everyone else."

"Oh, well good then. You learn to kick, girl, because you have to defend yourself. But having a good head on your shoulders is even better than knowing how to kick. Thinking about things, watching your back, not being one for romantic nonsense. Look, as a rule, if you like a guy a lot, it's not in your best interest, that is a sure thing. And I'm telling you because I know a lot about it. But, of course, one never learns from another's experience. You have to have your heart broken two or three times before it gets into your head. Young girls are crazy. Passionate. I was, too. And I paid for it."

She had finished transferring the cheap whisky to the brand-name bottles, and she rinsed the syringe and put it away.

"I'm not saying anything else because I don't want to."

She took out a rag and began to dry the counter. She wiped and wiped the same spot with the cloth, thinking about something else.

"Like the thing about Portuguese's son. So cruel and heartless. Because there are tragedies, and there are tragedies. And then there are great, total calamities, the kind from which you can never free yourself ever. That's how it was for Portuguese's wife. Just like a ghost. I had never seen anyone who looked worse. Like a crazy woman when they arrested her. With her eyes like that, with her hair in tangles... Of course I'm not surprised after what happened. They're worse than animals. Even a dog cares for its litter with more affection.

"They arrested Portuguese's wife?"

Rita looked at me with surprise, "But didn't you hear? It was some weeks ago already... A little after your uncle came back and that son of a bitch escaped... And no one talked about anything else in the Neighborhood... So you don't know anything then?"

I shook my head no. Rita bit her bottom lip and kept looking at me with a pensive expression, wondering if she should tell me the story or not. I waited patiently, convinced that she would tell me everything in the end. She liked talking too much to keep quiet.

"Well, it's a horrific thing, and you won't be able to sleep later if I tell you. But okay, it's how life is. It's better to know everything so that some cruel, heartless person doesn't catch you for being naïve and foolish. The fact is that Portuguese left, and a few days later, they took Portuguese's wife into the station. It seems that someone had reported them because the boy that they had, you remember, a baby of just over one year, well the baby had disappeared; he was no longer around. And they looked for the child all over, and finally the woman confessed that they had murdered him; and that they had buried him in the abandoned fields next to the new park. They did it on exactly the same day as the new park had its grand opening when all the hot shots from the city came. You remember that? And they went to the place where the woman said, and they removed the remains. It turns out that they buried the poor little thing alive."

She took a glass from under the counter and poured herself a half shot of the cheap whiskey that she had been transferring. She drank it in one gulp, coughed, and cleared her throat, "It's truly, absolutely terrible... And you didn't know anything about it...?"

"No."

I couldn't tell her—not even Rita—what the first few days after Segundo's return had been. A couple of flies fried loudly in the blue insect-killing lamp above us.

"Well, Chico knew it, I'm sure. I believe that's why he ran away. Chico took off when he heard about what Portuguese had done to his son. I say he was afraid Segundo could do the same to him. Stupid, because no one buries a grown child alive; he makes too much noise. They only bury babies alive."

Rita took the jar of black licorice sticks and began to turn it upside down to take out broken pieces, sweet bits and morsels, the factory mistakes that always came with each shipment. She made a little pile on the counter in front of her.

"Then the woman explained that the man had forced her to do it because he thought the boy was not his—the manias of crazy, bad men. Now it appears that the crazy one is her, and I'm not surprised. They've told me that they nabbed Portuguese—in I don't know what city—and he's in jail. I hope that they drive an iron rod up his ass. In any case, things must not have gone well for Portuguese with the captain. You know which one I'm talking about? The one with the gray hair. Because they said that guy has had loads of problems for leaving prisoners in shreds. They call him the Hammer."

She pushed the licorice scraps toward me.

"And for that reason, for being as violent as he is—and for all the problems he has had because of it—that's why they assigned him to the Neighborhood. Go on home now, take the sweets and leave. They must be waiting for you at home. It's funny... to think that we're the captain's punishment."

CHAPTER TWENTY-EIGHT

Since Grandmother died, Segundo had not left the house. He often went down to the club and locked himself in the dressing room for hours. But he never stepped outside again. He no longer did his show of illusions with the dwarf woman, and the club remained closed day and night. To my surprise, it looked like the entire place was ours.

"Do you think the seasoning spell that we put on him is taking effect?" Amanda asked the dwarf woman, whispering, full of hope.

Segundo was a different person – silent and absent. He barely ate, and he had noticeably lost weight in a short amount of time. His clothes were very baggy, hanging on his shoulders, which now seemed weighed down and bony; his face had lost its fleshiness and its animal force. Now skinniness carved out his high cheekbones, and his eyes burned large and dark over his considerably longer nose. Segundo didn't look like himself, but like someone else—maybe his deceased father in that portrait with his eyes wide open, that Grandmother had on her table before the fire.

"Tell me, do you think that he's under my influence?" Amanda insisted.

And the dwarf woman observed Segundo with a scrutinizing eye and answered, "No. It's not that. It's that he's waiting."

That's how the days passed, and we all were waiting: Segundo and I for my father, Amanda and Chico for Airelai to put together enough money so they could leave, and the dwarf woman for her good Star. For he who waits, days creep past -- slow and clingy. The hours are fused together in a colorless jumble, and the only thing that remains in memory is the raw pain of want. For that reason I scarcely remember anything about those final days. They are a gray cloud in my past. When I look back at that time, I only see myself one way—it's always the same, in the little square near home, seated on the ledge of the half-finished fountain that Grandmother liked so much, watching the end of the street, contemplating how the minutes were turning the corner.

At night, I barely slept. I went to bed and turned out the light, but it was like a neon sign had been turned on inside my head. It was impossible to close my eyes, to rest. The nerves in my body were like webs of fire. On my back I clutched the edge of the narrow bed as the darkness spun in front of me. I was missing something; something was pursuing me; something was hurting me. They were tense days and anguished nights -- the days and nights of the end.

That was when I began to sneak out of the house while everyone was sleeping. I waited until Chico was lost in the deep breathing of dreams, and then, by feeling around in the dark, I got dressed in the clothes I had left at the foot of the bed. I went out on tip toes; the hall was so dark that you could notice no visual difference if you closed your eyes. But I knew all the corners and each step by heart, and I could avoid the tiles that wobbled or creaked. I opened the door and took the metal that Amanda always left inside the lock so that no picklock could force it open. Then, I went down the stairs and came to the worst part: crossing through the closed club to get outside. I went on without seeing anything, not even the shadow of my fingers a few inches from my face, but I knew that now the club's bleak enormity extended all around that blackness. And my greatest fears fit inside that immense and immensely dark space. I passed through the shadows as fast as possible, without breathing, until I finally reached the club's door and burst outside, to the relief of the open air and the light of the streetlamps.

I was no longer afraid of the night or the street, or they only produced a relative fear in me—the wise fear that is necessary for survival. I remembered my arrival in the Neighborhood with Amanda, and the panic induced by those red doors and lights, and by those muttering men who seemed ready to devour us. Now I knew almost all of them by name: this one was the Monkey, the one who was crippled was the Ace, this one with the nose that was so big and full of hair was Paco Pipas. I also knew that they were, in fact, all dangerous, bad, crazy men like Rita said, but also men with customs and regulations that they usually respected. If they ran into me, I was ready to follow all the rules – to be humble and obedient. But above all I tried not to let anyone see me. I was small and thin, and I knew how to slip into the shadows.

I wandered around during the wee hours of the night, always watching the horizon to see if an outsider arrived. I covered the main streets, the ones that were necessary on the way to cross the Neighborhood, and when the sky began to fade into a dirty gray line near the roofs, I went home to bed. And then I slept, the sleep of the dead, without dreaming.

I always avoided Violet Street, the one with the bright glow in the windows and that veered off as a short, wide street, perpendicular to one of the main streets in the Neighborhood. Airelai, Amanda, and Grandmother had forbidden me from walking down it, and I didn't set foot on it for many nights. But Grandmother Barbara had died; the house had burned down, and Segundo didn't even see us. I'm saying that the world had changed so much that the old bans were beginning to seem too old. One night I came to the edge of that secret, appealing street, and without stopping to think, I took one step forward, and then another. I stopped, looked around, and determined that I had already delved into the first meter of Violet Street, which wasn't really called Violet Street. I read the street sign that was nailed to the wall, and it said Rose Street. The lit windows began a few meters ahead. There were some cars, not a lot, parked next to the sidewalks, and lots of men walking slowly in front of the windows. I didn't like those men; there was too much light and there were too many people, and they would see me, and perhaps get angry with me. They would say, "It's forbidden for girls to be on this street," like Grandmother Barbara, with her thundering voice, had told me, a long time before.

But now that I was here, my curiosity was unbearable. The street extended straight for a short distance before me dropping off into a downhill slope. The area with the lights didn't span much. I could probably cross it in a hurry, as if I were running some errand, looking for medicine for my dead grandmother before any of the men noticed me. In fact, while I was thinking about all this, a couple of guys turned onto the street, passed by my side in the shadows, without even glancing at me. That made up my mind; I clenched my fists, took off, and launched at a good clip down the slope.

In four strides I reached the lit area and entered it like someone who dives into a pool—I was a little surprised that I didn't hear splashing. I blinked, blinded and stunned by that distinctive violet light, which overtook the faces and objects, soaking up everyone's and everything's color. It was a livid, heavy air; movements here in the light seemed slower, minute, and endless, as if in slow motion or part of a nightmare. I looked around: glassy eyes, a cheek muscle trembling faintly, a finger raising slowly in the air. The men on the street didn't see me; they were all concentrating on looking at the walls. And on the walls, there were large, ghostly windows—gleaming display windows that opened from small rooms, and in each small room—bathed in the neons' black and blue light—there was a woman who smiled at the men on the other side of the glass, or they made gestures at them, or they ignored them,.

Some women were wearing very shiny, black plastic straps, straps that were knotted around their throat and full of spikes and coiled around their legs and surrounded their breasts exposing their nipples. There were others with very short, satin shirts of various colors—perhaps red, green, or yellow—all in tones that were flooded by that violet radiance, and they were somber red, light green, and dirty yellow. They sat on small, upholstered arm chairs, or on lacquered chairs, or stools, crossing their legs and showing their extremely pale buttocks. One of the women was the fattest person I had ever seen. She had blond hair with black roots, purple lips, and a quilted bathrobe that was too small for her. Seated as she was on a couch, she opened the robe and showed a large, trembling breast, as big as a wheel. In her little room, there was a floor lamp with a checked shade; a neat and cozy little kitchen; a fake fireplace with a plaster cat; a calendar with a photo of a dog and a girl on the wall; a table with a toaster and a few cups, as if she were in the middle of breakfast. But the cups were all clean. The giant woman opened her massive legs, and at the end of the fleshy tunnel of her thighs, you could see a black tangle that she was caressing. Some man near me on this side of the glass howled, and the sound reverberated and became distorted like sounds under water.

Images seemed to be distorted as well; the reality that I saw was hazy. The men were sweating a violet colored sweat even though it was not hot, and my steps echoed on the pavement as if the ground were hollow. There were many large windows on both sidewalks; some were closed with the drapes drawn. But in the rest, all kinds of women were strutting about: blonds and brunettes, young and old. A daze of roughed lips, blazing clothes, and tangled hair. And so, so much flesh. I thought I recognized a few under the heavy makeup: women from the Neighborhood who Chico brought coffee to in the afternoon. But not the large woman, not her. I touched my forehead, and I felt feverish, but my skin was cold, a little damp.

I had nearly passed through the whole street when I saw her. Her small room was decorated with Asian silks – they were very lovely cloths, and I knew then, even though here they had an evil, almost fetid color. She wore a gold belt, hung low on her hips, from which a drape of crystal beads was hanging; aside from that, she wore nothing. The first thing I saw was the lovely belt, and the silks in the background. Then I recognized her size and profile. Airelai was seated on a tiny little chair with her knees squeezed together and her hands leaning on her knees. Her body was very small and dark. I had never seen her naked before. She had breasts.

Like Amanda's—who I had indeed seen naked—but smaller. Breasts looked very strange on her girlish body. She got up and leaned one foot on the chair; she opened the strands of crystal beads, and a triangle of bronze colored flesh, with a split in the middle, appeared. She was like me; she didn't have hair. Buga had spurned me for being hairless, but now a fat man, who seemed somewhat drunk, approached the window and licked the glass with his pink tongue.

Then Airelai saw me. She lowered her head and met my eyes. I wanted to flee, but I couldn't because she was looking at me so strongly. At that moment a completely bald old man banged on the door that was next to the window. The dwarf woman went and opened it. A gust of warm air that smelled like sandalwood came out from the small room.

"Not today, Matias," Airelai said gently putting her hand on the man's chest.

"How come? Why not?" he said with suspicion.

"Look, I have a visitor, and I wasn't expecting her. I can't tonight."

The old man turned and looked at me. He squinted his eyes and laughed.

"But there are two of you! I didn't know there was another. Even better; I'm staying."

"No, Matias! She's not like me; take a good look. She's really a girl."

The old man looked at me again with a stupid expression. He furrowed his brow with worry.

"Yes, yes she is indeed!" Turning to me the dwarf woman scolded, "This is not a place for girls, Sweetheart..."

"I know, I know. I didn't know I was going to come here, I swear." I wimpered

The guy sighed, and then he cupped my cheek gently. He did it affably, but it made me feel sick.

"Okay, okay, I'll go. But I'm coming back tomorrow!"

"Of course, I'll be here waiting for you."

"Good night," the old man muttered and went off hobbling down the street.

"He's a good guy," noted the dwarf woman. "We were lucky. Come in."

She grabbed my arm and made me come up the stairs and enter the small room. She closed the door behind me, locked it, and closed the curtains immediately. She turned toward me, crossed her arms over her bare chest. Her eyes were blazing.

"If they see you with me, they'll take away my license and probably put me in jail. What the hell are you doing here?"

I had never seen the dwarf woman so furious. I was dizzy, and I felt nauseated. Inside the small room with the curtains closed, the air was an incandescent violet color—a poisonous, unbreathable air. I tried to speak, and I heard the deafening buzz of the electricity from the neon lights. Then, I opened my eyes, and I was on the floor with the dwarf woman over me.

"You've fainted," said Airelai with a calm voice. "Don't worry. You're okay now."

I still heard the neon's hissing, but not as loudly.

"That light..." I complained.

"Yes, it's terrible, right?"

The dwarf woman had put on a cherry red silk robe and had climbed onto a bed full of cushions that was next to the wall. I sat next to her. She was very serious, and somewhat sad.

"Why did you come?" she asked.

I shrugged my shoulders. "I don't know."

"Did you follow me?"

"No. I didn't know."

"What is it that you didn't know?"

"That this is how it was. That you were here."

"What do you think I do here?"

I looked at her. Something dirty, I thought. Something dirty, terrible, and moist. Like that fat man's tongue.

"I don't know."

"Answer me."

"Roll around with men. Dirty things."

The dwarf woman sighed.

"I am working. It's not the best job that a woman can have, but I make money. And with that money, Amanda and the boy will be able to leave. How did you think I earned all the cash that I bring each morning?"

"I don't know. I thought you did spells and magical things."

The dwarf woman laughed and lit a new sandalwood stick in the incense burner. It smelled a bit like Grandmother to me, like Grandmother Barbara's room in the first house.

"Something similar, in fact. I bewitch men. I practice illusionism because I put illusions in their heads... or a little lower."

She laughed again.

"I make them want me, and I fulfill their desires. Is there any miracle greater than the fulfillment of a desire?"

I didn't answer because I didn't understand the question. And because I knew that she wasn't talking to me but rather to herself.

"But no, you're right; it's a dirty job—ugly and disgusting and sometimes dangerous. Even though you make good money, better than other places. And, hell, there are worse things, I assure you. In the end, I'll stop once I've raised enough."

"I know where there's money. A lot of money," I murmured.

"Oh yes?"

"Segundo has it. A suitcase full. He has it hidden in the dressing room. In the closet with the spotlights. You have to take everything out, the tiles and everything, and take out a board that's in the back. And there is a hole with the suitcase."

"So it's there," the dwarf woman said pensively. "So close the whole time."

She shook her head decisively, "But that money won't help us. We can't touch it. It's blood money, and it belongs to someone. Amanda can't use it to leave, so I have no choice but to keep working in the window a few more nights."

I took a bit of her silk robe in my hands. It had a cold, soft feel like the crystal ball that hung from my neck.

"Airelai..."

"What?"

"Airelai, when Amanda and Chico take off... you won't go, right?"

The dwarf woman sighed and rubbed her face with her open hands. Then, she leaned toward me and looked me in the eye. "Don't worry," she said gently. "I'll stay with you until your father returns."

CHAPTER TWENTY-NINE

"I know why Chico ran away from home," the dwarf woman told me one day. "And it has nothing to do with what you think." It was time for an afternoon nap, and the two of us were in the kitchen, I was making cutouts with the pages of an old magazine, and Airelai who just gotten up was having coffee and toast. She had placed a mound of cushions on the chair, like she always did, so that she could reach the table top. The dwarf woman had organized her life very well to compensate for being so small in stature. She tied long twine to the latches and windows, for example, so she wouldn't have to stand on tiptoes to open and close them. She had a lovely, small wooden stool, painted red and with a whole on the top board to grab with, and that she used to get up on a chair or to reach something. This time, nevertheless, was different though. She hadn't gone to look for her stool, which perhaps was in the dressing room downstairs, but she had extended her up arms out to me so that I could lift her onto the chair. I gulped the air, put my arms around her, pulled her with all my strength, and set her on the cushions with ease. She didn't weigh anything! I think I blushed because it was the first time that I had picked her up. She, on the other hand, looked very calm. Airelai finished her mug of coffee, got settled on the pillows, and she began to talk:

"It happened one morning, shortly after Segundo came back. I saw Segundo go into Grandmother Barbara's room and close the door. He was in there a long time, perhaps half an hour or perhaps more, and I could hear the indistinguishable murmur of their conversation. At the end, I heard yelling at Segundo, "But what more do you want me to do? I freed you from that guy, and I did it, me, alone!" There were a few seconds of more guarded whispers, and then Segundo left the room abruptly, his face flushed. He went to the kitchen, grabbed the bottle of cognac and collapsed onto a chair. But he didn't drink. To tell the truth, he was completely sober. He remained still for a while grabbing the neck of the bottle, staring blankly at the wall.

"I was in the kitchen, and Chico, who had been caught off guard by his father's entrance, was too. The boy had been playing with his matchbox cars on the floor, next to the window. When he saw Segundo arrive, he became extremely nervous. I could see that he wanted to leave the room, but in order to do that, he would have to walk dangerously close to his father. Also, he was behind Segundo's back, so he must have thought that he could go by unnoticed if he remained still and didn't make a racket.

"Some time passed like that without any of us moving until Segundo, without changing his position, said loudly, 'Chico.' The boy started was flustered but didn't do anything. 'Chico,' his father repeated with a calm voice, 'Come here.' I saw how the boy became pale. He stood up and went around the table, slowly, trembling until he had situated himself on the other side of the table across from Segundo. Then the latter cleared his throat and rubbed his large hands together uncomfortably; his knuckles cracked like dry wood. He looked at his son and smiled. Segundo smiling! I think that was the first time I had seen anything like that. Chico must never have seen it either because his expression became even more frightened. 'Come here,' Segundo said patting his knees with his hands. The boy took a very short step forward. 'Here,' he repeated, and Chico dragged his feet one more step. 'If you want, I can tell you a story,' Segundo said, and the boy remained rigid, clutching the edge of the table with both hands like a bird. 'Don't be afraid, come here, and I'll tell you a lovely story,' insisted Segundo, still smiling. Chico moved a tiny bit toward him; half a centimeter—almost nothing, the smallest advance imaginable. 'Look, so that you feel comfortable, you can choose. If you want, you can go, and if not, if you stay with me, I will tell you a very fun story. Tell me, what do you prefer, to stay or to leave? Come on man, answer, no one is going to do anything to you...' The boy turned his head bashfully toward the door. 'What do you say? What do you want? Go or stay?' Segundo insisted cheerfully. 'Go,' stammered Chico in a nearly inaudible tone. 'And if besides telling you a story, I give you this money?' Segundo said, taking out a bill from his pocket and showing it to the boy happily. Chico repeated, 'Go. Please.' And then something terrifying happened. Segundo kept looking at the boy, and he began to cry. First they were round, silent tears, large teardrops that slid down his cheeks while his lips remained petrified in a smile. And then he collapsed like a popped balloon; his large heavy head fell over his chest, his shoulders slumped, and his back began to shake with the sobs. His face was twisted; his expression was hideous; the weeping was spouting out of his eyes; I never saw anyone cry like that. I looked at Chico; he had a look of disbelief and horror fixed on his father. I called to him, trying to calm him down, to soothe him, 'Chico,' I said to him. 'Chico, don't worry,' but the boy didn't even hear me. Suddenly he seemed to recover his ability to move. He took off from the table, running from the kitchen with the quick agility of a squirrel escaping danger. And the next morning he left home.

"I haven't told anyone this story until now, and perhaps I shouldn't have told you. I didn't tell Amanda because she wouldn't have understood anything: not the reason for Segundo's tears, nor the flight of the boy. You don't understand either, but since you're a child, not understanding does you no harm.

"Adults, on the other hand, cannot bear not understanding something. They are not capable of accepting mystery, and they invent thousands of stupid explanations to fill the void of what they do not comprehend. They grab onto those foolish explanations like fanatics, the more stupid the explanation, the more blindly they defend it, and they even kill for them. They slit throats because of their fear of the void and their mistakes.

"I have known Segundo for a long time, since those distant years when I worked in his father's magic show. He wasn't an ugly young man. He was always different from his brother, even physically. Segundo was broad and stocky; Maximo was tough and bony. But the two were tall, good looking guys. Maximo looked more like his father; he even had blue eyes. Segundo's face, on the other hand, always reminded me of the face of a dog, with that moist, powerful snout. I'm talking about before, long ago, when he hadn't lost so much weight, when his eyes were not sunken, before they had slashed that horrific scar on his cheek. It was then, long ago, when he met Amanda, when he won her heart. Perhaps he was a good man then; well, I don't know, with that crazy face that he had later. Men are an enigma to women—just as women are to men. Males and females are like distinct, secret planets that spin slowly through the cosmic blackness. Sparks fly when their orbits intersect. "Love is simply the pressing need to feel one with another person, to think just like that person, to stop suffering the unbearable loneliness of knowing that we all live and are condemned to die with. And so, what we seek in the other, is not who he is, but rather the simple illusion that we have found a soul mate. We believe we have found a heart capable of throbbing in the maddening silence in between our heartbeats, while we run through life, or life runs over us, until we're finished.

"I'm going to tell you something else that you don't know. We, the Lilliputians, are the direct descendants of Paradise. Do you remember that sepia colored photo that's in my trunk? The one of that little tiny woman with the ruffled skirt? She's Lucía Zárate, my mentor. When she was already very old, she taught me the secrets of our religion, our hidden knowledge. Just as I have taught it to other Lilliputians and will teach it a number of times more. Because as you already know, we have great longevity. Lucía's picture dates back to the end of the last century, but she managed to live until my time. However, she must already have been an adult woman in the portrait: let's say thirty years old. Remember how she stands on a round table covered by a fine, dark-colored tablecloth with gold trim. The wall in the background has wide, richly carved paneling. It must be a public place, perhaps a music hall or a small theater. I know they used to show her, like an exquisite rarity, in the variety shows. Lucía is very proud in the middle of that table—proportionately perfect, admirable, her very fine, elegant body poured into a close-fitting suit with a frilly neckline, the ruffled skirt adorned with fringe that was perhaps deteriorating. She must have gone through great financial hardships. Then there's her beautiful head, her dark ringlets over her ears, her youthful, round cheeks ... and those eyes. Lucía Zárate has a sad, old before-her-time look on her face. I don't know if you've noticed, but we Lilliputians are sad. I can just imagine the scene at the moment of the portrait. There are no chairs or stools near the table, so someone, out of necessity, had to lift her up in his arms. Perhaps her patron, the one who exploited her in fairs and small theaters; or maybe it was the photographer. I suppose the photographer asked the dwarf woman to smile; standing behind his box, under his black cloth, for the woman to smile for the portrait. But Lucía posed with her bitter mouth shut tight and her eyes distressed. When I met her she was already blind; I never had a chance to see that look from the photo in her eyes—so blurred and desolate, so terrible.

"Lucía was one foot, eight inches tall. Just one foot, eight inches—from her black curls to the tip of her Moroccan leather booties. So I'm quite a few inches taller than she was. Experts say that she was the smallest human being ever in history: maybe so, maybe not. The records of height have only been kept systematically during the past century, and we know so few famous Lilliputians from past eras. Like Soplillo, who kept King Phillip II company during his adolescence; who, as we see in Villandrando's painting, was a dark young man with a thin, delicate and beautiful face. However, he was a lot taller than Lucía, since he must have been about thirty-one inches. Let me remind you that we Lilliputians are not ordinary dwarves: we're tiny beings, but we're perfect in every way. And that perfection, as I told you before, is the trace and legacy of Paradise.

"I know the little people's law, and I'm educated in the ancestral ways, in the hidden knowledge of the Beginning. That's why I know the origins of things. Before time existed and before the Fall, all the Earth was an Eden. Our ancestors, the creatures that lived in that happy world, were double beings composed of one enormous, very strong giant who always carried a delicate, beautiful dwarf riding on his shoulders. Both partners lived in perfect symbiosis, in the most complete spiritual communion. They had no need to speak to each other. For that very same reason, the Word did not exist. The colossal one brought stamina, boldness, intuition, and sensuousness to the couple. The Lilliputian contributed intelligence, imagination, and sensibility. They were immortal, and they were both sexes. I mean gender did not exist. They were male giants and female giantesses at one and the same time, dwarf men and dwarf women. I don't know if such angelic beings are even within the grasp of our imaginations today.

"There were a lot of these double beings—so many in Paradise—but they just barely paid attention to each other; they were engrossed in the inner beauty of being soul-mates. They were satiated; having the other was enough. Each Lilliputian went with a colossus, riding astride on his hefty neck. Both enjoyed total intimacy. They never felt alone, nor misunderstood, nor lacking for love. They walked through Eden's gardens, admiring the panthers with curved claws; the multicolored birds; the tame bears; the dazzling suns that were never stifling and the fragrant rains that barely wet. The days were always quiet with the sweetest possible moments.

"I told you once that time didn't exist in that original world: everything took place in the same indefinite sigh. That's why, since there weren't mornings or nights, hours or minutes, memory didn't exist either. Our ancestors lived in a continuous present without recollections or plans. That way, they were happy, with a happiness that I don't think we can imagine today. It was pure and limitless—the absolute joy of innocence.

"But there was one couple that believed theirs to be a special union. Maybe it wasn't true; maybe they weren't any more or less united than the rest of the immortal beings. But what's important is that they thought they were. Mainly, it was the dwarf, who thought about his giant, thought just like his giant, and felt complete because their relationship was so perfect and beautiful. The dwarf loved his better half so much. He was so happy with him, that he began to experience a strange uneasiness: the desire to recall all those sweet moments that they spent together. The dwarf tried with all his might. He attempted to etch those joyous moments in his mind to remember them. But all of his work was useless, because once it had been lived, life faded away. Until one day the dwarf came up with a strategy. He grabbed some dry bark and dye from a berry, and he painted the scene that he was living with the giant on the under side of the bark (they were swimming and sunbathing in the rivers' pools).

"The trick worked, and that moment became a little memory that remained in the Lilliputian's mind. The memory burned inside his skull. It burned, stung and throbbed inside him there. Other memories were being added to that first one: big, sticky blotches of different memories that formed a shapeless ball. The more his memories grew, the more disturbed the dwarf became. Now he delved into those joyous moments that had already passed, comparing some with others, and it seemed to him that the present was not as beautiful as what had already been. Then he began to feel a new uneasiness, as if he had a bird caught inside his chest, a large bird that didn't have room to spread its wings.

That dark bird was shifting about under his ribs—leaving the dwarf breathless—until finally all that pressure took shape and rose to his mouth. It was a desire. The dwarf wanted the giant to demonstrate his love for him more clearly.

"The intense heat of desire was completely new to the Lilliputian. So he carried his desire on his lips for a while, thinking it over, gnawing at it without knowing what to do with it. The desire was giving off a tart, acidic juice that seared his tongue bit by bit. Until in the end, all wounded and aching, the dwarf shed a tear. He grabbed onto the giant's locks, hard, and let his desire out. It trickled out, hissing through his lips, and made him say the first words on Earth, 'I want you to tell me that you love me.'

"Then the skies ripped open with an awful thunder. The birds fell to the ground, dead. The panthers slit the throats of the lambs. The rivers were dyed with blood, and the horizon was devoured by the first night. I mean that's how we lost Paradise, not with all that nonsense about the apple. The Word is what made us wretched and human. From then on, time began to escape us. There were no longer any double beings, but just poor, scared, lonely people like you and me, incomplete beings, looking for the soul mate that we lost. That's how the sexes came about, as evidence of our humanity —that is, our limitations—like a stigma for mutilating the other. That's why, when we love, we do it so desperately, because we can never possess or understand our loved one as we giants and dwarves of Eden mutually possessed and understood each other. We are no longer complete, but rather, just one piece.

"People don't usually remember this beginning of things; the timeless era in which we were together and happy. But as our torment, we Lilliputians do retain this memory. Perhaps it's because we are still too close, genetically, to those tiny people of Paradise, or because the first dwarf's error is punished in our flesh. It is a cruel punishment, I assure you, because there is nothing as heart wrenching as remembering that joy and knowing it was lost. It is that painful emptiness that burns in Lucía Zárate's sad eyes. Do you remember the photo? She looks so alone standing on the table, hopelessly longing for her giant. Because she knew, just as I know, that there's no way to redeem ourselves after that fall from grace. Nor is there a soul mate who can break through this nightmarish iron fence that surrounds each one of us. All we have left is to go on riding astride our own death."

CHAPTER THIRTY

The fountain's pond had a ledge made of gray, rough concrete which was wide enough to sit on. It was there where I planted myself to carry out the long hours of my wait, gazing at the descending line of the street and the passing of people. I memorized all the marks and crevices of all the old houses surrounding the square, places where the plaster peeled off in the shape of a dog, a palm tree, or a mill; I studied how the sun moved along, coloring the sidewalk on its trajectory through the sky, how it sniffed around entering and exiting the doorways, how it trickled down the dirty walls disdainfully and lit the fake stone fish that no one had ever placed in the middle of the pond, and which was now definitively broken, split in half, exposing the iron re-bar in its guts.

One day I was seated there, after eating, in the late afternoon, when the sun was weighing down on me, and the Neighborhood slept. I was alone and lazy there; nothing moved in that still hour, not even the wrinkled papers that had accumulated in the gutter. Half asleep, dazzled by the light, I saw him appear down there at the end of the empty street; his whole body had a misty bluish color because he was in the shade, and the sun, which was thrust onto the pavement one meter beyond him, was too blinding. The man walked up the sidewalk at a steady pace, wrapped in the darkness and in a strange calm. From the first moment I saw him, even from so far away, I knew that he wasn't from the Neighborhood. My heart did not beat faster; I didn't breathe more deeply. Everything was written, and in my head there was no room for any anxiety or any thought. At that moment, I was nothing more than my eyes that watched. My lungs, my heart, my kidneys, my brain, my liver, all the other parts of my body, were simply the tranquil biological support for my fixed gaze.

He continued up the street, and I began to hear the sound of his walk ringing out in the silence. A large man, I could see now, he was large and blue, bathed in the shadows. He was half way up the street, and he was looking at me, too. There was no one else in the world except for him and me. I was very still, and the man moved forward with his footsteps echoing like a heartbeat; his height became more obvious as he reached the top of the slope. He was now very close, but he stayed on the dark side of the street, in that liquid twilight of late afternoon, and his face and body were still a sliver of the night. One step, then another, now he was in the square. Two more strides and he crossed the shadows like a rocket and came into the sun. The light fell over his shoulders like a waterfall, and painted colors on him from head to toe: brown shoes, light gray pants, cinnamon colored sweater. A tall, thin man with broad shoulders, long arms and legs, large bones. His eyes were deep and calm and never wavered from my face.

He arrived in front of me and stopped. He shifted the gray jacket that he carried to the other arm. I remained seated on the ledge of the fountain, and he gazed at me from above. Now I realized that it was he who Segundo looked like after he had lost weight. The same pronounced cheekbones, and that long nose that Grandmother Barbara also had. But those features, which seemed so disproportionate, heavy, and even brutal on Segundo, were solid and refined on my father. He bent at the waist and leaned toward me; his eyes were blue and so sweet.

"It's you, right?" he whispered softly. "You must be Baba."

The sun went dark and lit up again, and the universe cracked with a great roar in my head, repositioning itself, like the repositioning of a dislocated bone with one painful pull. I saw faces that I didn't realize I knew, and a laughter full of white teeth that jingled in my ears. Bright rooms, a flowery bedspread, a woman's hand tickling me. I smelled an extraordinary, warm scent -- the scent of kisses and shelter. I remembered for a moment that I had been happy, and then I lost that memory again immediately. I had burst into tears inconsolably, but I didn't want my father to think I was a crybaby, so I swallowed my saliva and said:

"Yes."

"And do you know who I am?"

"Yes."

He looked at me for a long time in a way I cannot explain. Then he extended his right hand, with the fingertip of his index finger, delicately touched the crystal ball that was hanging on my neck. Then he lifted his hand and brushed his finger along my cheek, the most gentle touch. He smiled lightly.

"Now I have to go," he murmured.

"I'm going with you."

He shook his head, no, in a friendly calm manner. He was an enormous presence over me, a protective shadow.

"You can't come. I have things to do, things that are very serious."

"Please," my eyes filled with tears.

He looked at me furrowing his brow, pensive, and distractedly touching the scar that he had on his face – a white, somewhat sunken, very thin line that went across his right cheekbone.

"I tell you what we're going to do. I'm going to go now and settle all my business, and you wait for me here until I return."

I hiccupped a little.

"Look, I'll give you something in the meantime," my father said with a happiness that was a bit forced. "Something interesting..."

He took out his wallet and looked through it until he found a small photo that he handed to me.

"Take it. You can keep it now, and then give it back to me... It's a photo of your Grandmother..."

I put it in the pocket of my skirt without even looking at it, still crying. My father sighed and straightened up.

"Don't be that way, Baba. It's just a little while."

"Come back," I begged him.

"I promise."

I saw him walk steadily around the pond with his steady walk, head toward our street, and turn the corner. Before disappearing, he didn't turn around to look at me; I thought it was a bad omen. I bit my fingernails trying to figure out what would be the best course of action for me. When I finished with my last finger, I got up from the ledge and went after him.

Our street was empty, but I guessed that he had entered the club. I pushed the door stealthily, the least amount possible, so that the glare of the sun outside would not give me away. I stayed for a few moments in the small entryway defined by the threadbare hanging velvet drapes, and I waited until my eyes got used to the darkness. Voices could be heard on the other side; I opened the curtains and slipped into the club. It was dark except for the main stage lights, which were dusty, weak spotlights recessed in the ceiling. And on the stage, under that direct, feeble light, Segundo and my father were arguing.

"It wasn't me, Maximo, it wasn't me."

"You're a coward."

"I'm telling you it wasn't me. Why don't you believe me? It was an accident. A short circuit."

"Of course. And the second fire, too. You're a coward. And you're crazy."

My father's voice was scarcely more than a sharp whisper; while Segundo was yelling and moving his arms in the air. He was pacing nervously on the stage, not taking his eyes off his brother who was resting against the wall at the back. My father was pale, and his scar was even whiter, like a thin ashen line that crossed his face. Segundo's scar, on the other hand, was swollen, shiny, and red—a revolting, slimy being, a shapeless sea creature stuck to his cheek.

"What do you want with me? Why did you come?" Segundo shrieked trembling with hysteria.

"Where is the money?"

"What money? For Christ's sake, Maximo, it burned up!"

"Remember I saw you."

"In the second fire! It burned in the second fire."

My father spit on the floor.

"You disgust me."

"Why do you treat me like that? Why have you always treated

me that way? It's not fair. And you don't know me. You don't know me." He stretched his hands in front of him and lowered his voice, "I've killed. I have killed. You should have more respect for me. And more fear. I am a dangerous man."

"You killed her. I know. That's one of the reasons why I came," whispered my father in an icy voice that I found disagreeable.

"No! No, no, no," shrieked Segundo again. "That was an accident. A short circuit. Holy Christ, Maximo, you've never let me live. Why are you after me?"

A small hand clutched my arm, and a furious little voice exploded next to me, "What the hell are you doing here?"

It was Airelai, a strange Airelai with blazing eyes.

"I... My father... That's my father, Airelai..."

"I already know that, stupid!" roared the dwarf woman.

I looked at the stage; Segundo was twisting his hands, and my father gazed at me harshly.

"Leave," he told me with that icy, terrible voice.

I burst into tears.

"I'm sorry... I didn't want to..."

"Leave, Baba," my father said again, more gently now. "Don't worry. It's okay. Go to the pond, and don't move from there; I'll come to find you in a little while."

Airelai pushed me lightly toward the door.

"He got furious with me," I said, crushed.

"He didn't get furious. I know he didn't. You'll see. Go to the pond and wait for us," the dwarf woman comforted me.

Before I could think twice, I found myself blinking outside, blinded, with the club door closed behind me. I walked wearily toward the square, worried about my own blunder. There were some kids drowning a lizard in the fountain. I sat on the concrete ledge in the same place where I was before, only now I was looking the other way, toward the corner where my father would have to appear. The cement's rough surface scratched my thighs, the afternoon was heavy above my head, and that's how the hours began to pass ... slowly.

CHAPTER THIRTY-ONE

Later, long after my father died and everything ended, Chico and I were together and alone, at home in the new house while the winter was clenching us from the other side of the windows. He told me what had happened in the club that afternoon.

"I was there. I heard the shouting from the house, and I went downstairs. I was there the whole time. I even saw you, and I saw how they threw you out. I was hiding on the stairwell behind the curtain. You should have done the same thing; you were so dense to stay there in the middle of it all, like a fool. You know, looking through the crack between the curtains, you can see the stage perfectly. A bit of a sideways view, but very close.

"When you left, the dwarf woman said, 'I know where the money is.' Hearing her, Segundo began to scream, 'What money, what money?' But Airelai didn't even look at him. 'It's in the dressing room, in a blue suitcase, inside the secret compartment that's in the closet,' she said very calmly. 'Are you sure?' Maximo asked. 'I just went to check.' Then Maximo approached his brother and grabbed him by the lapels, 'And what story are you going to tell me now, what do you have to say now...' But he shut up suddenly because Segundo had put the tip of a huge knife on his throat. I don't know where he had taken it from, but there it was, a large hefty knife like the ones my mother uses to cut meat. And he leaned the tip on Maximo's neck and laughed, 'What do I have to say now? Well, now I say this is another matter. Right? Now you respect me more, right?' Maximo didn't move. He didn't say anything. He was still and rigid. 'With a little more pressure, just a little, goodbye, poor Maximo...' Segundo said, and he let out a burst of laughter that sounded awful. 'But I have a better idea; now we're all going slowly to that back closet, and you're going into that closet with your dwarf woman, and I'm going to lock you in, and I'll leave with my money.' 'And you'll set fire to the place before you go, like the last time,' Maximo said in a calm voice. 'What a good idea! I'll have to think about it...' answered Segundo.

"Then the dwarf woman began to walk. She took a step forward and then another. Segundo looked at her astonished, and then he shook the knife near Maximo's neck. 'Don't move! Don't take another step; I'll kill him.' But Airelai said, 'No, you won't do it,' and she kept moving forward. 'I'll kill him! I'm going to kill him! I'm going to slit his throat!' screamed Segundo. But the dwarf woman reached them, and pulled a chest close and got on top if it while Segundo looked at her with wide eyes, frozen. Then Airelai got up on her tiptoes, stretched out her little hand, put her finger on the tip, and pushed it. The blade retracted because it was one of the trick daggers from the magic act.

"Segundo turned very white and dropped the knife. Then, Maximo, completely calm, pulled something out of his back pocket.

The thing made a little noise, and then I saw that it was a switchblade, and he had just popped out the blade. This one was certainly real, it was a thin, dangerous blade that induced fear. Segundo looked at Maximo and Maximo looked at Segundo, with the knife gleaming between the two of them. But Maximo didn't make up his mind to act; a few second passed, and everything stayed the same. 'Do it once and for all,' the dwarf woman said. 'Segundo wouldn't have hesitated so much; he had Grandmother Barbara's pistol, and he was waiting for you to kill you, but when I saw that you were coming, I stole the piece from him.' And then the dwarf woman took Grandmother's small silver pistol out of her pocket. Still Maximo couldn't make up his mind. 'If you don't' kill me now,' Segundo said with a very hoarse voice, 'If you don't kill me now. I'll finish you off some day.' And I liked that he was capable of saying that. Maximo lowered his hand, closed the switchblade, and put it away in his pocket again. 'Let's go,' he said to the dwarf woman. Segundo fell to his knees, covered his face with his hands, and cried. The dwarf woman went to him, and touched his shoulder. 'Segundo,' she called. Segundo was all curled up, leaning on his elbows on the floor, crying forcefully. 'Segundo,' Airelai insisted. He lifted his moist face and his eyes met the dwarf woman's. Then the dwarf woman stretched out her arm, placed the barrel of Grandmother's pistol on Segundo's forehead and pulled the trigger. This all happened very quickly.

"The two went immediately to the dressing room to get the money, and I guess that is when Maximo left you that wad of bills in an envelope with your name on it. I saw them come into the club again, with the suitcase now, cross the room, and go outside. I thought about following them, but I was too frightened. No, that wasn't it—it was as if I didn't have the strength, as if my legs weren't my legs, and it disgusted me too. I couldn't come out from behind the curtain and be in the middle of all that blood. If I stayed behind the curtain, it was as if the blood were not real, as if it were a movie. So I didn't move from there. I remained still for a long time; I don't know how long—until my mom came and began to scream like a crazy person.

"Then, hearing from this one and that, I found out that Maximo and the dwarf woman had gone directly to the airport and had gotten on a large, heavy plane that was going to Canada. That was the plane that exploded that night as soon as it took off, with one hundred seventy-three people inside. I think it had something to do with the suitcase, or maybe there was a bomb in the suitcase. Why it blew up then, who knows. But the airplane exploded when it was still gaining altitude, and that's why it could be seen perfectly from the entire Neighborhood, a ball of fire that burned everyone to a crisp; that's why the Neighborhood smelled so bad, like burning flesh, for all those days after that. I didn't see the explosion because I was still behind the curtain, but they've told me that the sky became completely red with the explosion and that it was a horrific show.

"Segundo's head exploded too, and that I did see. It was a strange thing, because from the front, which was where the dwarf woman had shot him, there was only the bullet hole. But from behind, everything had come flying out. Pieces of head and blood and stuff. What we have inside. The stage and walls were splattered. That's why I couldn't come out from my hiding place. Because everything was covered by him, everywhere. I know that he was my father, but it didn't matter to me that they killed him. Only that after they shot him, everything disgusted me, and I felt dirty. Now I'm better, and I'm happy Segundo doesn't live with us now. Anyway, I liked that he said to Maximo, if you don't kill me now, I'll kill you. He was afraid, but he wasn't daunted. I liked that about my father, and I'm nothing like him, but you never know."

CHAPTER THIRTY-TWO

The sun went down behind the roofs of the houses; the sky became white and then gray; night arrived with silent steps, and the lights came on by the fountain. From where I was, one couldn't see beyond the beginning of our street; I was dying to at least go to the club door and watch for him to come out there, but I didn't dare disobey him again. My father wouldn't love me if I did. I still remembered his look from hours earlier when he told me to leave - his eyes stern and furious. I had dreamed of his arrival so much, I had yearned for that moment so much, and now I found myself worried and confused, distressed by my awkwardness, fearful of having let him down. I closed my eyelids because the street lamp was spinning. With all the excitement I hadn't eaten; maybe it was that. But I wasn't hungry. I just had an emptiness in my stomach and in my chest – an emptiness as large as the dark night.

I opened my eyes, and the streetlight had become still. Better. Some boys crossed the square and looked at me. They were the ones from the Botines gang, and it was already the third time they had walked by that evening. They weren't some of the worst, but they weren't good people either. Now they didn't scare me in the least because nothing could be worse for me than the fact that my father didn't love me, and that unbearable dread crushed my heart and drowned my mind, leaving no space for any of my other fears. So, scornful, I returned their look and they went away, down Broadway kicking a tin can along.

Something soft and warm rubbed against my legs. It was a male cat, no a female, perhaps one of my Grandmother's pets. The felines had scattered after the fire, and we hadn't seen them again. But this little affectionate kitten seemed familiar to me; I scratched her chin and lifted her face. Those triangular ears with white spots on the tips, the light gray and white stripes on her back. She was very thin, almost bony, but without a doubt, it was Lucy Annabel Plympton.

"My dear Lucy, it's been so long since I've seen you..." I said out loud, scratching her scraggy belly. And then I added, because Grandmother Barbara always wanted us to repeat their full names, "Lucy Annabel Plympton."

The cat purred, delighted. I remembered perfectly the afternoon that we had seen her name in the cemetery. It was a very old gravestone, split in half with mold in the cracks. "Lucy Annabel Plympton, 1882-1900." The inscription in the stone said, "Lover of trees, wind, water, birds, flowers, and friendly beasts." The cat was a friendly beast, who now stretched and rolled playfully on the ground. So Lucy was about eighteen years old at the time of her death. What was death? I already knew what death was. I had seen Buga and my Grandmother. It was not seeing, not smelling, not touching, not being. It was disappearing forever and ever. A vertigo, a fear greater than that of the darkest stairs, or that of crossing through the club in the shadows. But that only happened to other people. I couldn't die; I was a girl. The cat licked my ankle, meowed once and left running.

Then I remembered – I don't know why – the photo my father had given me. How could I have forgotten it during all that time? My hand trembled with excitement when I took it out of the pocket of my skirt. It was printed on thick, hard and yellowing paper, not like modern photos. It was a pale dark brown color like the photo of the dwarf, Lucía Zárate.

I looked at the image in the light of the street lamp. It was a girl more or less my age with curly, tousled hair flowing in the wind. Hadn't my father said it was a photo of my Grandmother? But it didn't look like Grandmother Barbara. The girl was thin and strong; she was wearing some kind of knee-length cotton slip with lace, and that was blowing in the wind also, and some socks – just socks, no shoes – all bunched up at her ankles and perhaps wet. The bottom of her slip seemed drenched, too, the fabric sticking to her right leg. The girl was standing on the fine sand of an empty beach, and behind her one could see the darkest line of a foamy sea. She was looking forward and smiling, happy and proud, wrapped in that damp breeze that must have smelled like summer and fish – high eyebrows, almond eyes, round chin. An icy hand clenched my stomach; she didn't look like Grandmother Barbara, but like me. The girl wore a glass bead on her neck. My glass bead, the one my Grandmother had given me, with the same tiny, cloudy spirit frozen within the glass. I lifted my hand to my chest and gently felt the sphere; still, it was cold, as always. The girl wore the bead's chain like I did – doubled up; it must have been too long for her, too. Behind her, the sea was shining, reflecting a sun that wasn't in the photo. There was an inscription in the corner written in ink that was a little runny with a childish, round handwriting, "For my dear Dad from your little Baba."

I put the photo in my pocket and pushed it down forcefully against the fabric at the bottom until the old paperboard cracked under my fingers. That girl suddenly bothered me. That picture my father had carried in his wallet, that wind, that sea, that stupid inscription. I took the photo out again; it had become crinkled, and a few wrinkles appeared on the back. I leaned over the fountain's pool: a few inches of black water, crushed beer cans, broken glass, floating plastic debris, a child's shoe stranded in the middle of the basin on top of a mess of dirty rags. I opened my fingers and let the picture drop. It stayed on the surface with the wrinkled part face up. I splashed the water a little with my hands, creating a light current that took the photo toward the center of the fountain's pool, like a tiny boat. There it began to list little by little; the paper must have been soaked. The tiny boat was sinking in the wake of light painted by the street lamp over the putrid water, just like the sun painted gleaming trails over lively seas. I thought of my father wondering if what I had done to the picture would bother him. But he had given it to me. I looked toward our street; it was dark and no one could be seen on the corner. I looked at the photo, and it was no longer there. I sighed and dried my hands on my skirt. I kept waiting.

I had spent an immeasurable amount of time seated on the hard ledge, and my back hurt. I stood up and walked a little. Without realizing it, I found myself on the corner of our street. From there, off in the distance, you could see the club's door. Closed tightly. My own recklessness frightened me. I didn't want my father to find me spying on him again, so I hastily walked back a few steps. I was standing in the middle of the odd intersection, far from the corner and from the fountain, in a no man's land where the light of the street lamp barely reached. My face burned there where my father had caressed me with his finger, as if my cheek had been sliced, my skin wounded. Above my head was a round and liquid sky, a placid lake of black air sparkling with stars. They sparked in silence above me—beautiful, cold fires—and I was the center of all that abundance of energy. The dark warm Earth, asleep beneath my feet, sustained me.

Then it happened; then the miracle came. I heard a stampede at my back and the entire sky turned red. I turned around, and there it was, at the edge of the night booming and crackling as if to announce its arrival, alight with colors, a flaming and powerful mass, even more beautiful and impressive than the photo in the trunk—it was the dwarf woman's Star.

I recognized it right away. I knew that was it; it couldn't be anything else— the magic Star of Happy Life—a blinding ball of fire that devoured the darkness. The Star boomed again and suddenly exploded into a thousand smaller stars, bright embers. I witnessed that golden rain, enraptured, and I saw tears of fire fall one after another and go out in the shadows. Finally the sky cleared; the air became calm; the blackness of the night pooled up again. I remained, trembling, in the middle of the square, which now seemed so dim and ugly after the miracle. The neighbors were talking with great excitement, leaning out of doorways and windows, not knowing that what had just happened, had happened for me—that what they had seen was my Star, which had come from distant astral skies to show me that life was sweet and that wishes are always fulfilled. Someone watered some pots of geraniums; a sheet of drops fell on the ground.

One could breathe the plants' intense, green smell. Above, in the recently calmed night, a gentle and lazy half moon sailed in a small sea of clouds. So much life ahead and all mine. And so, peaceful at last, I returned to the jagged ledge of the fountain, and I sat down to wait for my father to return.

Born in Madrid in 1951, **Rosa Montero** has been a journalist for Madrid's daily newspaper, *El Pais*, since 1976. She has published eight novels, many of which have been bestsellers in Spain. Montero's novel *La hija del canibal* (1997) won Spain's most prestigious literary award, the Premio Primavera de Novela.

Adrienne Mitchell is a literary translator and tenured professor who holds an M.Ed. in Educational Leadership with a focus on second language acquisition and pedagogy, as well as an M.A. in Romance Languages from the University of Oregon.

Aunt Lute Books is a multicultural women's press that has been committed to publishing high quality, culturally diverse literature since 1982. In 1990, the Aunt Lute Foundation was formed as a nonprofit corporation to publish and distribute books that reflect the complex truths of women's lives and to present voices that are underrepresented in mainstream publishing. We seek work that explores the specificities of the very different histories from which we come, and the possibilities for personal and social change.

Please contact us if you would like a free catalog of our books or if you wish to be on our mailing list for news of future titles. You may buy books from our website, by phoning in a credit card order, or by mailing a check with the catalog order form.

Aunt Lute Books
P.O. Box 410687
San Francisco, CA 94141
415.826.1300
www.auntlute.com
books@auntlute.com

This book would not have been possible without the kind contributions of the Aunt Lute Founding Friends:

Anonymous Donor	Diana Harris
Anonymous Donor	Phoebe Robins Hunter
Rusty Barcelo	Diane Mosbacher, M.D., Ph.D.
Marian Bremer	Sara Paretsky
Marta Drury	William Preston, Jr.
Diane Goldstein	Elise Rymer Turner